www.burningbookpress.org

boys, Bedouins,

and castratos

boys, Bedouins, and castratos

a novella by

Jeremy Sanders Nichols

The Burning Book Press
Washington, DC

THE BURNING BOOK PRESS EDITION
DECEMBER 2003

Publisher's Cataloging-in-Publication Data
(Prepared by The Donahue Group, Inc.)

Nichols, Jeremy Sanders
        boys, Bedouins, and castratos : a novella / by Jeremy Sanders Nichols.

             p.   cm.

        ISBN 0-9748280-0-9
        (formerly ISBN 0954379691)

1. Men--United States--Psychology--Fiction.
2. Masculinity--Fiction.   3. Frustration--Fiction.
4. Political alienation--Fiction. I. Title.

PS3564.I34 B69 2002
813.54

Manufactured in the United States of America

PART 1

Chapter 1

The sand on the street is hot and working. It is a salt plain. It is a vast salt plain, stretching for miles, and it is working; drying the sweat from my shirt; drying my lips and the collected blood. I can taste it on my tongue, as I can taste the midday sun baking, like an oven, this salt plain. My right hand is buried in the sand. It is limp and across its beaten knuckles that protrude through the grains as four camels' humps/ the cast shadows of circling airplanes in descent; I am overlooked on this abandoned salt plain.

I am without a signaling-flare under a yellow sun hanging 90 degrees to the horizon and I am alone; my right leg is broken as I cannot move it and the pain in my skull is so fierce that I breathe shallow, but it is this loneliness/ and the sun bleaches color from the landscape and the sand stirs under a warm breeze.

I lift my eyes, blackened and red, to the distance that undulates with my blood's pulse; it moves, like aggressive thoughts, through the backs of my eyes. I, however, cannot move. My head rests heavy with the weight of so many missed hours of sleep, but my eyes will not shut.

Mirages rise and in their flame-like flickering- Bedouin screams; I hear screams of Bedouin women rise from the pavement; across the pavement; beneath the blinding sun, charging toward me in cavalcade without stallions, and I smile because the rubber bullet did not leave me deaf, and the stampede has not the hoofs to crush me.

The sun has burnt the day into an underexposed reel of film; the figures are unclear, and the injury to my head only complicates matters. The Bedouins emerge from beneath the yellow sun, as if from the corner of a smokers' lounge; enshrouded in cigar smoke and applying kohl liberally in shadows. Before I see them clearly, I hear only their voices and the clanging of medallions that adorn their coverings.

...But I am mistaken.

And it all seems incongruous.

The Bedouins are jean-clad boys.

The Bedouins are jean-clad boys and the clanging of medallions are the clanging of swords that prove too unwieldy for the boys and the salt plain is a street; a hot and working street covered in sand; carried from the hills on the soles of the vendors' feet.

They are out of sight, perhaps watching from the surrounding hills that emerge now from the corner of my eye, much like a player who, having exited too early, awkwardly makes his return to the stage. The vendors are listening to the cries down below; to their chanting; their Bedouin cries shrill beneath their palms. My parched throat refuses to lift up again and I, as well, am audience to my Bedouin sisters.

(Was it the immersion? The bleeding of salt into the wounds as I slept without dreams on a vast salt plain? Should my sisters now seem so foreign, delicate, and absurd?)

They flood the street, kicking up sand in their wake, polluting the air/abrasive/sand paper breaths drawn deep that irritate the lungs and certainly the officers' patience-they are in the street; the police are here in the square.

Behind shields, helmets, batons, gas masks, tanks, projectiles, and the law the police protect our right to assemble. And I hate them for this; they are clever and fatly satisfied; soft pink in the status quo; they will only watch us, the Bedouin. They are clever. You must incite them to violence. You must incite them to censor. Their greatest weapon is their passivity-it whispers authoritatively, in stolen moments behind the backs' of grooms, into the brides' ears, "Speak, boys. Your words are not deadly. You are free to speak. We are the ones that must watch what we say. Our words are heavy and would crush you."

I am audience to the Bedouins. They dance without me, as I am lame. They sing without me, as I am dry/barren/and my throat is hoarse.

The square they gather in lends itself to the occasion; it is a cathedral with a skylight drawn open, and their voices resound through the valley with presence. The lyrics are lost, perhaps as the Bedouins speak with a strange tongue, but no matter really the substance is in the melody and the boys have nothing to say. But their voices! Their voices, they reach the hills

…And for its impotence, it is a lovely sound.

We castratos sing lovely songs. They must give us that. And they do. At intervals in the open-air service, faintly there is heard a silent ovation from the hillside; the vendors and men of politics commend our youth with the dull striking of canes and the patting of fleshy, sunburnt thighs milked from the bottom of Bermuda shorts. But we are boys as we are castratos as we are Bedouin.

We are men singing with the same terrified pitch with which we called our mothers to our bedsides late at night, as there are stirrings beneath our garments as beneath our beds/ terrible monsters, and these stirrings drive us mad with fear as we cannot take them in hand, as there is nothing to master.

I am lying on my back now. My face has stopped bleeding. The sun is casting shadows, and the silent ovation falls thick, like huzzahs on so many palm leaves that the Bedouin/castrato procession seems little more than a passion play   delivering a predictable end.

The sky is a clear pale blue, like the Madonna's robes. On my back the boys, silhouetted against this baby blue backdrop, look almost swathed and infantile as they whirl dervish around the square. Every choreographed move tumbles them deep into the sky's cradle. Every syncopated step and finely executed turn draws them furiously together, as a nursery of Siamese twins all looking to one mother.

They are looking to the Movement.

And as a real mother they exhaust her, as they sustain her.

Their behavior is reminiscent of a too young child, not yet weaned, tugging at its mothers blouse unaware that she guards the secret of her double mastectomy, and here, from the street, I see that the boys and I are very hungry.

(And here from the street, am I seeing why?)

We are tugging at mother's blouse, as we have always done, but today I see that we are fed from the bottle in the refrigerator and by the hand of our father that now pats his thighs, in commendation, as mother dons the middle-management uniform, as she is self-conscious enough to not look poor, but too poor to look rich.

There is a sharp pain in my head, and there is a sharp focus to my eyes.

The singing and the chanting and the banners will disperse together, as we have never learned to be alone. Our lot is cosmopolitan in its provincialism; it is everywhere and everywhere it is thought unique. When the night comes we will all cry though with the same fevered pitch for the breast we have never seen; we have never learned to be alone. We are kept company by these impossible thoughts of a full belly, fists pumping furiously from the Movement's teat everything our appetites crave. But the Movement? She is nursing only her surgical wounds.

The State is duly noting.

The State is marking every defiant gesture, like a courtroom stenographer, recording in short hand the much labored over mandates of the Movement and her Party. The State is scripting concessions for when the Bedouin boys will be called to the Table. Papers will be drawn and men from both sides of this capoeira conflict will return to their homes satisfied for having struggled to no end. The boys will receive a weekly stipend for candies and cigarettes and the State will have the peace of mind of a well-ordered household at heel.

The Table is forever unacceptable. Shoddily constructed, it is supported by three legs and though re-formed every hundred years it is constructed always on the same three legs that threaten to give. No matter what style the Table takes it always threatens to give. There is rumor that it in fact collapses when all parties rise to leave the room, but no one has seen this. To hear the old men talk no one will ever see this.

"The Table must collapse," the boys sing.

It rests always precariously on the lap of the State's grandfathers and old men have notoriously weak knees. Already they are shifting in their seats, straining under the weight of the Table and the realization that they could, (with more ease than I, myself, could hurl a stone) send it all careening to the floor; the papers, the concessions, the absurdity of open mouths making inarticulate sounds. The grandfathers are impatient and the castratos in the square are singing lovely, like their granddaughters. And this, perhaps, is why the grandfather's stomach their discomfort, reclining with groans and crackling bones that twist, as leather, to watch our pageant from the hillside, and do not send the Table to the marble floors, freshly waxed, before they send it to the furnace.

The grandfathers could so easily bring it all to collapse and beyond; they could bring it to nothingness. A single anarchist in their ranks and the Table could pass from the roof of the capital to the basement where the books are burned and the book burners employed. But they do not. They hold to their ground and the Table stands, and the boys are permitted the luxury to believe that the grandfathers haven't a voice because they do not sing and the Table's collapse could be their design.

The Bedouin boys are piling petition upon petition on the wearied men's knees, as the Table "must collapse." And, like paperweights, rocks are hurled through the grandfathers' windows. They gather, as if on a scale that never tips in the castratos' favor.

...Like shards of metal piercing my temples, these thoughts of mine awaken me to the protest, as they drive me further, in a banishment of sorts, from my comrades/from the boys. The street becomes once again a salt plain, where overhead the commercial airplanes make their final descent, circling the control tower, and I want nothing more right now than to be carried from this street, this salt plain, these thoughts that sting my eyes to tears and rupture my heart in an arrest of conscience/ I am at my birth and the yellow sun, hanging 90 degrees, is calling me to walk a road unfamiliar.

(How am I to walk when I know my own leg is broken? And I am starving?)

The castratos pull me into the belly of the crowd, and I am secure from the authorities and martyred without a sacrifice; the boys around me are incensed. Appropriately enough, they break into a dirge.

"Bastards!"

"Look what they've done!"

But no one remembers the officer's face. I have wrestled with the faceless and am injured for the effort. And in the mass confusion, the officer has bled into the Wall, the wave of uniformed humanity. He has bled into the furthest ranks; into the radios inside the buses brought to transport the vandals; into the commands uttered through these radios and through the men on the other side. The officer is faceless. The officer is everywhere.

And all around me, only the moon in the sky has a face.

The throngs of boys are a forest of humanity; a protective copse, but really only a field of grain for a field mouse, and only the farmer at the thresher's wheel has saved me in this golden sea in which only the sky penetrates. Still, the moon is in this sky; in this still pale blue sky without a single cloud and for its presence the air is cooler and the street, once a salt plain, is simply a street warm to the touch.

In my delirium, in this confusion, the face on the moon, however shifting, belongs to the moon and running my fingers across the bridge of my nose reveals the foreignness of my own features and I am lost without the Movement that starves me and the boys that sing me to sleep.

The boys, the singing boys, are talking.

"Take him to a hospital."

Young man, why are you so lovely?

"We're taking you to hospital. Do you understand me?"

..."I don't understand anything."

"Take him to the hospital!"

So lovely. Why are we so lovely?!! Why do we sing like the ladies? Why do we preen our feathers, fine peacock, colors of rebellion? Today...today my red breast reveals hollow sparrow bones.

"Take him to the hospital!"

Why are we so lovely?!! Why do we stand pretty in the square, banners in hand, on display as if the State were a curio and the sun no more than artificial light to play on our delicate lladro faces? Why? Why are we the States sprezzatura? Ineffectual as the feminine disarray of a well-tossed blanket; draped across a complimentary bedspread? Are we nothing more than subversives?

"Get this man to a hospital!"

"Nothing more than subversives."

"Goddamnit, a hospital!"

At the birth of the State, boys, there was our opposition. And before there were words I had something to say, but before the Movement?

"He's blacking out."

Strange, I thought I was waking up.

Chapter 2

The hospital room is a corridor. Ochreous light floods the length of the corridor from unreliable ceiling bulbs. The walls are a wise Goethe yellow; there is no conversation. Men play chess and stare idly into the expanse of the room. There are no partitions and everyone's business is everyone's business.

An ill pallor affects us all, as there are no windows to be drawn, no sunlight to wash the illness away, and the circulation of air is very poor.

I can smell infection. My brothers are rotting; a fact that elicits only disdain. I keep these thoughts to myself.

There is a particularly fierce chess match taking place across the way from me. I recognize one of the men as a protestor, and, as there are no guards standing round, looks are exchanged; that peculiar commiserate relief.

He is losing his match.

He is losing his match to the middle aged man with a leaky catheter, and every pawn, knight, rook stripped from his board drives him further into his already pronounced self-righteous indignation. His gestures grow more frantic. He grips his head frequently, drawing his fingers across his shaved temples. His language is more obscene and pointed. With the queen's loss, his loss, the protestor hurls a bucket of vitriolic language at the elderly man's face, and for those who remember courtesy- it burns like battery acid.

But for those who think- the young
protestor has never known the rules of the game.
The young protestor does not even know it's a
game.

He is still in the city square, amid the
singing and the chanting. His displaced
mannerisms reveal this. He undulates with the
serpentine motion of a crowd though he is alone,
even as I am across the way.

My leg is broken and recently set, and I
cannot move with him, though I feel that this is
not the only reason I remain…restrained.

I watch. I watch as the old man with the
leaky catheter, nurses the young protestor to
consolation. The phrase, "it's only a game;
we'll play again later" acquires a mantra like
significance, and though there are no windows
every patient in the room hears the lightning
outside; experiences the maternal affection of
the old generation to the young and winces for
its ugliness.

We are all not so blind under plastic
light; the old man with the leaky catheter is not a
mother and the young protestor is not a boy
frightened of a storm.

And for many of the boys chess is a
game.

The young protestor is crying.

He is crying in the arms of the old man.

The old man is crying.

He should not cry.

Old men should not cry. It is ugly. Like
beasts of burden with paralyzed hind quarters;
lumbering about on two legs; naying and stirring

the dust around them before collapsing to the ground having made nothing but a terrible noise.

The stench is overwhelming.

"Open a window!"

"There are no windows."

There are no windows to look outside. Nothing to distract my attention from this unnatural sight; this rotting pieta; from the spectacle of this old man, impotent and incontinent for his non-virginal existence, resting a supine self-professed maligned castrato on his exposed chest; nursing him to a breast that is not there; still pulling sour milk. And the game of chess is just a game and the protest, and its pageantry, and the loveliness of our voices-all a theatrical game.

I turn my head to the wall. The odor of the obscene exchange will stay fresh in my mind.

My leg is pulsing in its cast, making it difficult to think, and I must think.

Because I don't understand.

The old man weeping, like a bruised little girl and the young man suckling; piglet; raised for the rendering plant; tusks torn from his jowls long before he could ever miss them. Perhaps this is why he sits stupidly working his mouth, as though chewing cud; he is running his tongue across the absence of his boar tusks. He is now just a pig, just a piglet, and the absence is a cavernous memory of what was once and is now unknown. A memory a stone's throw away, yet acoustics and the echo mar remembrance. It is a burning appetite; no matter how many delicacies are laid across the Table for the young protestor's consumption his round barrio eyes, hungry for the meal, will turn on you and demand, dumbly, satisfaction; his is the ignorant appetite. He is Hemingway's fish; suffering not from the hook, but its ignorance of what has him, and what is making it very hard to breathe.

And this ignorance racks his temples, as his fists beat his brow, as his generation's autism attacks the old man with the leaky catheter.

The young protestor turns quickly. Perhaps he's seen his reflection in a bedpan; seen the sour milk running down his chin, soaking his hospital smock and his hairless chest. Perhaps the old man mistakenly said something soothing. It's possible; something contemptuously treacherous against the Movement; against the boy's Movement. Perhaps this is why he smiles at me before his hands tear at the old man's side and his fists beat the old man's pasty white face. His words are indiscernible. They are a torrent of incomprehensible dissatisfaction. They are the poetry a neglected east European orphan would compose in its cradle as the nurses continuously walk past it; smokes in hand and boyfriends on their mind. His words, his inarticulate rage, are confrontation with the cruelty of an indifferent universe he has not the talent to negotiate into the sublime, or the money to afford its escape. He can only rage, and rage furiously.

The old man collapses.

The young protestor is eventually subdued by a team of male nurses. Sedated and restrained; he has never stopped mumbling. His words are barely audible. The entire corridor, like gossipy hens, is straining to hear them. Some claim to hear the Party line. Others hear comments of a faithless lover or a domineering father. From across the way, I hear only the mumblings from the underground spring of frustration; breaking through the earth at every opportunity.

I hear the frustrations.

I hear the frustrations; the incommunicable frustrations of a peculiar place in time; the frustrations of a generation born on the Author's death; born to be no more than a convergence of circumstances; delivered indiscriminately to the arms of a biological mother or the sterilized pan of refuse in the clinic, wherein we are conveyed to disposal …to be resurrected at a later convenience; resurrected without god or a faith in resurrection even.

I hear these frustrations in his every swallowed syllable; in his poor annunciation; in the Party line he tows in between his drugged self-reprisals and his flattering portrait of a dog he remembers wanting as a kid, but that his father' second wife wouldn't allow.

My leg is pulsing madly. I can think of nothing else; it won't allow. I am listening to my pain, and as the young protestor drifts off into addiction, as the medication is very good, my thought is of the Party line and a bathroom stall, in which a young girl hides bulimic.

I am tired, and the primacy of this urge vexes me so much so that I am compelled to reach into my belly with my left hand, tickling the roof of my mouth where the throat begins and purge myself of everything; spilling onto the floor, the clean linoleum of the hospital floor, every expectation and principle I can find swimming in my stomach.

They are hovering around me. The patients; they are reading in the alphabet soup of my guts, exposed on the floor, my affiliations and hypocricies. My clean running automobile and the Saturdays I pour toxins into the sewers; the young ladies I've married in my mind, while I courted another for decorum. They are reading, from my deep recesses, every clandestine action and ill motivated act; every stone thrown for the Movement, though aimed at my poor self-opinion. Repulsed, condemnatory, transfixed, and familiar not a hand is raised against me. Someone fetches a mop, bucket, and wet towel for my face and hands, soiled for the effort.

The patients stand.

The young protestor is asleep and the old man is dead.

And I am light with the weight of realization.

"Hypocrite."

"Leave him alone."

"Those are my guts."

"Don't you care anymore?"

"Can't you read?"

"No, I can't."

"…don't you care anymore?"

I turn away. I am tired. I turn away from their faces. I turn a deaf ear to their conversation. I turn my back to their

remonstrations and the hands extended in
sympathy. I turn away. There is nothing there.

In their faces, the intimations of fathers
and mothers; the boys whose faces light up
familiar, like a childhood friend; the effeminate
boys with the soothing voices that quiet the
frustrations, but never subdue; I turn from these.
I turn away and withdraw; leaving behind
memories and education; indoctrination and
cohersion; loyalty and the refined culture that
determined me, but no more. I am tired.

I withdraw into myself. I feel as a
vessel on an open sea.   Again.   I was here
before.   All accoutrements that adorned my
person are discarded. The banners, the chants,
the identifications; all compass to who I was and
believed myself to be…

…my vessel is an iron hull and these
compasses do not work here.

Chapter 3

I am released into an overcast day. It is
late morning before the businessmen and women
will flood the streets in search of something to
eat. The vendors are plagued by scavenging cats
thrust on them by their callous owners; they
accommodate them all; they've no other choice;
the cats are everywhere.   They infest the
garbage, whether sealed or not. They climb on
the chairs and tables, hissing at customers,
leaving their dead kittens at the their feet as
indictment for having not intervened in the back

alley, out of sight when the teenage boys stoned them to death and then drank themselves sick.

It all seems so familiar, as I turn the last corner from the hospital to the open square still littered with debris and the remnants of yesterday's demonstrations.   The piles of discarded clothes and banners, slightly stirring in the breeze, intimate a western ghost town; heightening my sense of alienation, or at least bringing it to my attention.

I have left the dance floor. The music is over and the incessant hum of the rhythm and bass passes with every minute till I hear clearly, and I hear nothing.

It is overcast and there are no bearings to be got by casting my vision to the heavens, so I simply stand. There is nothing to see, save the swirling of clouds threatening rain and a humid night under a ceiling fan that will not work without the lights on. The heavens tell me only that it will rain and I hope that the exhaustion of the past days will carry me through the discomfort of sleeping in my own sweat.

I am not alone in the square. There is a young woman arranging café chairs for the expected patrons.   She is dark haired and roughly my own age, perhaps slightly older. I do not remember having seen her before, though I know I have. She has served my friends and I as we discussed "logistics." I would stand tall in my seat when she would ask for our orders and if not I would certainly own my indifferent airs; I was a man possessed of himself.

As I am neither hungry nor thirsty I will sit down and have her wait on me as my leg is broken and reminds me with every step. That I have gotten this far is testament, though I cannot say of what.

I am pleased that her shop was not damaged, and I tell her this. I am worried as she walks away that I was misunderstood. I will make my sincerity clear when she returns with the drink. She does not return. Instead a young man has taken her place. He is nice enough and apologizes for the waitress having to have left. I except his apology and ask if everything is all right. He says yes, but does not elaborate. I ask for the check and leave. I did not finish my drink and my leg seems well enough to walk the distance home.

It begins raining. I am fortunate to have made it home before the heavy downpour and am only slightly damp. I undress and recline on the bed with windows open awaiting the humidity.

I will call into work tomorrow and apologize for today. It is easiest to make an apology than to make an excuse; I am not a good liar and they do not want to hear the truth. They do not want to hear that I am relatively at ease and they are relatively inconsequential to this ease. Each paycheck I receive tells me that I am as equally inconsequential.

I tried once for a raise. I worked quite hard. The days grew longer and the more competence I demonstrated the more work I was assigned until soon I could not sleep and I dreaded the expectations; if hell is not other people than it is certainly their expectations. The pay raise did come eventually, but the

increase was not worth the effort and soon I
returned to my own routines. They objected, at
first. They asked, as is customary, if I were well.
I said, truthfully, that I was quite well and I even
thanked them for the concern, naively. But soon
enough their thoughtful inquisitiveness revealed
ulterior motives and my more than typical habits
became imbued with a "saboteurs" persona; I
was in their eyes lazy and was dismissed after
several warnings. Since then I have been
terrified of being perceived as anything less than
mediocre. I have my station and I know it. It is
somewhere between my appetites and what I can
endure.

The light of the ceiling fan makes the
entire room so painfully clear. The head wound
that bled rivers into my lungs; my broken leg; its
steady stream of air clears away the baron's "fog
of battle," like so many spiders' webs. The
world is painfully clear when not in the
demonstrations. It is all so painfully clear-

My protests are a day of fools? They are
the fools' days when king is servant and servant
king and my demons are exorcised so that I
might return to work tomorrow, but the king is
never the fool and he never leaves the hillside
and I never leave the stage and the turning of
cartwheels, like a ceiling fan; I am always the
organ grinder's monkey and the player in the
square.

I am always the fool and always on
stage. And these thoughts, these thoughts and
not the humidity, will stop me from sleeping.
Under the ceiling fan, in the mid afternoon, my

leg pulses with straining blood, and I sweat profusely in the humid air; waiting.

"Are you sleeping?"

A woman's voice.

"No."

"Your leg is broken."

"Yes."

"You can wash dishes with a broken leg."

"Yes."

"You're not working today?"

The woman is my sister, and the child by her side is my son. He is four years old and does not speak, but if ever he does he will call me uncle and my sister mother. He will never know the well-intentioned arrangements that brought about his new lineage. He will never know his real mother; his real father's name; he will never know a father, but he will have me.

I should have left a long time ago. Before his eyes, wearied and alone, looked to me for guidance I could not offer.

If ever he cried it would be for this, this deficiency, like scurvy; it robs him of teeth, but he does not cry. Rather he sits stoically, as if at mass, pacified with a plastic cup of breakfast cereal. And when the cereal is gone he gestures towards his "mother" and the tiny cup is refilled. He has never gone hungry. Still though he should cry.

I once took him to a doctor, but they could not make him cry. The immunizations the State demands did nothing and though his reflexes contract for the sting they seem almost calculated as though he were working through his body on an indeterminate delay; he is conscious of the expectations, but he musters only a recoil.   He withdraws from the fire because he will be burned. He holds my sister's hand because he will be lost. He sleeps in the afternoon because we slept in the afternoon, but for no other reason. He is looking to me for something that I cannot offer and for my rudderless existence he is without direction and sits, stands, and sleeps through a cheese cloth haze; I wish this were an old movie.

I wish this were his doing; that he were an old movie star; finely tanned and ridiculously self-conscious. I wish that this were all his doing; the impenetrable haze and the hungry eyes with a full belly. I wish he were a movie star; a hero; a legend of the big screen and this were only a quirk celebrated as show biz eccentricity.

He is eerily pale. He looks like my sister. This is good.

And this is my doing.

I cannot believe this.

I am a convergence of circumstances; I am not responsible.

And he must be a show biz eccentric because I must sleep tonight.

"Look after him tonight."

She should not trust me, but the boy is well behaved and will not wander far if told not to wander far. He will sit down beside the bed and when his cereal is gone and he cannot wake you he will work the corners of the plastic cup until his gums are raw and he is tired.

I am exhausted and cannot sleep. The rain falls on the open windowsill. One of the stray cats, a tabby, is cleaning itself on the sill and she is at once inside and out, and the cleaning is exercise in habit and futility. I see her belly is descended.

The boy pays no attention. He makes no moves towards the cat to play with her or nudge her maliciously into the street below. He is not yet the teenage boys. He is looking only at me, and I am doing nothing. I am lying on the bed. I have not moved from where his "mother" found me. He knows what to think of this; you can read it in his eyes; he thinks nothing.

I feel almost compelled to grab from the floor a t-shirt or pair of socks, roll them into a ball and hurl them at the cat just for the boy to know; for the boy to do. He does nothing.

I do nothing.

No matter; soon enough and sooner than later he will feel a compulsion, like firewater in the bloodstream. One day he will turn his face from mine and follow outside that door a fine packaged derriere, and he will act. Ignoble.

If I'm going to sleep I cannot bother with this. I have work tomorrow and need my rest. I am fortunate that at least the tabby has not brought a dead kitten to my windowsill, unless of course they are dead in her belly, but she is not caterwauling and where there is no smoke...

"Isn't that right, boy? Where there is no smoke."

He does not answer. There are moments when I believe I see his mouth working to form a word, but to date the word is lost in the boy's ruminations. He has never answered me. He sits with his empty plastic cup in his lap, cradling his belly in his tiny hands, and stares.

He is like a Buddha.

And I pity his enlightenment.

"I pity you. I pity you. You're wandering door to door, aren't you? You are knocking and with the supplicant's hands. You are indifferent to the tabby on the sill; she is only a cat to you and not even that. She has kittens in her belly, dead or alive, and what matter is that to you? You are wandering door to door and with the supplicant's hands and they are not your hands; they are not yours. You are not broken. You have to stand to be broken. You have to stand with your face to the mob of uniformed men and rattle the Party line through chattering teeth on a burning summer day and then can you be broken. Then can you vomit your conscience on the hospital's linoleum for strangers to countenance your vanities and shortcomings for which you can never repent; then can you be broken, but not now.

"Goddamnit, will you beat that cat or feed her!

He has two arms; one is for compassion and the other cruelty. Boy...do something.

"...What are you waiting for? What do you need from me?"

Chapter 4

As the mattress is worn, the sweat pools. I feel as though I am fighting a fever; I imagine every bead of sweat that trickles down my now naked chest to carry with it traces of disease. It is a delightful prospect and not one I am keen to abandon, however untrue; I am not with fever and the dripping sweat is not the bodies response and defense.

I am simply without air conditioning and the sounds of the jazz musician that usually fills the night air.

I wonder where he is.

I look to the open window, but the ceiling fan will not operate without the lights. Only the pitch-black night, sharply contrasted against the artificial electric lighting of the bedroom, penetrates as an almost sublime black rectangle; I cannot see outside. I do not know where the musician is and I do not know why he does not play tonight, as the night is alive.

It is a night of midriffs and tank tops; children who should not be playing at such hours; stray dogs and cats; neglected doorways and occupied alleys; hard drinking machismos and the exotic, wandering, working eyes of the foreign ladies generations removed from home. The evening is his, as it is the young black boy with street shoes corrupted for tap dancing; I hear the tapping, but it is missing the songs.

The tapping boy misses the songs, the lyrical songs of the horn player. I am not one to romanticize. I am only curious, and my boy, the boy of my sister, is lying beneath a coat on the end of the bed. The boy sleeps like a sack of potatoes; he must wake again tired having not dreamt.

I uncover him; the night is too warm for a coat.

I use a hand towel to dry my wet back and arms, and throw on a wife beater without cologne. I am curious where the horn player is and don't have time for sex; in truth, I haven't an interest.

He is not far.

The horn player is hunkered down beneath a neon sign advertising a tanning salon; he is as black as purple.

He is hunkered down on the streets curb with his horn carelessly flung to the side. The mouthpiece is a few feet away and I must reach as I sit down to grab it. I hand it to him, but he says nothing and does not except. I hold onto the horn and in silence we sit, as the motor scooters, teenagers, couples, and old women out on their girls' night out walk by. We sit for hours; till the early day; before the sun's rise.

As I stand to walk away he says to me, "I am a black man and I play jazz."

I say, "I know."

I remember the boy at home, and I remember that if hell is not other people it is certainly their expectations.

A couple asks the horn player for a song.

I hand him his horn, and as I walk away, as I reach the foot of the stairs that leads to the apartment, I hear through the street a horn playing softly, low, and broken; the musician sounds tubercular, as if he were choking on his own fluids; at least choking something back.

It is too early to go home. The boy will sleep until my sister wakes him. I never set foot on the stairs. I walk away; down the street; toward the square; where the café innocently leaves always one or two chairs for the stumbling drunks to recline in until morning; the drunk will need a cup of coffee and tonight, or rather this morning, I will keep them company.

When the café opens its doors only I am left; the drunks' daughters were sent out to fetch them. They dragged their fathers away cursing them for their lecherous ways and predilections for waitresses at cafes.

The walk to the café strained my broken leg and I immediately ask if they've pain medication. The waitress says no, but offers instead a cup of coffee to warm the blood.

She is friendly. She thinks I am hung over for my appearance.

It was here. Here in this café, where we together as brothers orchestrated the demonstrations; filled orders for the paraphernalia; cultivated one another's good opinions, as we cultivated the respect of men in authority without authority. We played the general's role; barking orders and commandeering enviable tables in the café's window for all to see. We were young and potent and rallying, and those who passed by, who saw us through the windows and hesitated to enter for our stature, only reaffirmed our position.

Cigarettes were smoked and wine was drunk and our uniforms, the uniforms of the street guerilla were always to specs.

Unlike the practical attire of the jungle guerilla that serves a function, the street guerilla is always on display. A carnavalesque absurdity; he is brilliantly colored as though the cobbled stones of the pedestrian walkways were an Elizabethan theatre and it is always important that the Montagues be distinguished from the Capulets. If we wanted victory we would have worn billboards, but we wanted only to be propped in the café's window; we wanted to be the department store's mannequins, dressed to the nines in Che t-shirts and anti-polizei boots. We wanted to wear our labels on the inside where we could not read our own ridiculousness.

I last spoke with the brothers two days ago.

I am walking into the square; I have left something behind, and, like the scavengers following the American civil war, I am looking for a pocket watch clenched in the fist of a confederate soldier or the last love letter a union man wrote his wife; I am looking for something before the battle and I do not know why.

My footsteps carry me through the motions.

The sun is lingering on the horizon. The day is turning blistering hot and though my shadow is long the moisture from my back evaporates and the stones of the surrounding buildings are difficult to look at. And so my head hangs down to shield my eyes and my shadow seems to me as long as my face, though

I know I am not wearing an expression. I am wearing nothing for anyone to read, as expressions are like words, and I am standing dumb.

In the square, turning over garbage bags and empty fast food containers littered with protest tickers and the odd button; I am standing dumb when just days before I was singing.

"Were you there?"

The waitress; there are no customers in the café and she's the leisure to wander over.

"Were you there?"

"I was there singing."

"I didn't hear you."

It is strange that she says this, and I think for bit before answering a question she never asked.

"I was there singing."

"You were all singing together."

"I was there."

"I didn't hear you. I only heard your friends."

They aren't my friends.

"I wasn't there for friends. I was there for the cause."

She pauses.

"Still I didn't hear you."

She asks for money; I did not pay. I reach into my pocket and realize that when I left the apartment looking for the horn player I forgot my money. Or rather I forgot my wallet; I don't know if I'd money. She understands and starts a tab.

I'm not good for it, and I want to tell her this. I'm not good at lying. There are few things I am good at and I want to tell her this. I want to tell her everything and I want to convince her that I was there and perhaps that this is the reason I'm working through the square, and I'm not simply going through the motions of making and then collecting nostalgia.

I don't want to be a scavenger; a Yankee carpetbagger; a liar, but on my hands and knees working through the trash- I don't want to be here, but it's so difficult to want to be anywhere.

And somewhere between my appetites and what I can endure...

I am not hungry.

Chapter 5

The backdoor to the kitchen is always open. The homeless wander in on occasion and beg for food. They are quickly pushed outside into the side alley and beaten by the manager. He is a large fellow with a pronounced speech impediment. He is terribly embarrassed for this and rather than verbally assaulting the homeless men, as they would certainly blush at the first lisped obscenity, he resorts to violence; it is not unheard of to find two, maybe three, men unconscious lying beside the large green recycling bins outside.

The manager is a great proponent of recycling.

He insists that each glass is sorted to color and each plastic sorted to its number code found on the bottom of each bottle. Newspapers are bound and kept under the cash register in the same cubby as the Billy club he uses on the homeless and rowdy drunks, though the deli rarely sees but a few "inebriates" in the course of a year. That he has never been convicted of battery is testament to the silence of his employees and the morbid identification that comes from working for such a man; "I work for the deli;" and this is a distinction.

The manager notes my leg, but does not speak. I joke of having walked into another deli's kitchen, and because he does not respond. I am wary of him. I wrap the apron and wash my hands as thoroughly as I had been taught. The manager is a certifiable obsessive compulsive, washings his hands several times a day. I have seen customers abandon their orders as he was taking too long in preparing their food; he was preparing nothing aside from raw hands later in the day that bled at the knuckles. I have watched him working through his routine.

He will pull first a paper towel from the always-fresh stack of paper towels at the top of the dispenser. He believes the dispenser is filthy on the inside and so it serves only as a shelf and is never actually filled. Under this first paper towel which he discards into a special pile for recycling; a pile specially reserved for the young Mexican bus boy who touches only filthy dishes; he pulls a second towel that he drapes over his shoulder, so as not to soak the pile of towels when he returns to dry hands after washing them.

The washing itself is as equally ritualistic dependent on the number of customers in line. It is not uncommon for a healthy queue to endure a sizeable wait of perhaps ten to fifteen minutes as he works a single groove in the palm of his hand as though he were cleansing himself of his Mediterranean pigment. The loss of patrons is comical, as it can be nothing else.

Originally, I had tried to expedite his ritual with coaxing, but the more I detailed the size of the orders and the expectations of the customers the more methodical his ritual became and the more noticeable the counting; he counts each finger, each groove, each curve, each aspect of his hand, as though he were afraid of missing something, but he's not.

The young Mexican busboy explained it best and I agreed: and so these days I find myself counting the grooves in my palm and not the men and women in line. We will be out of business soon. I'm not worried.

Between orders filled I sleep and am woken by a gentle nudging of the busboy who delights more in the thrill of waking me to the kitchen than saving a job I am in no danger of losing. After all, I can keep a secret. I was there and I remember his face.

I cannot forget his face. And I cannot forget how quickly it was bundled again behind a bandana- the manager has a new cut below his eye; he has a new song in his heart, and I know; he has a few stones in his pocket.

• • • • •

Before I'd hurled the stone that returned a volley of rubber bullets, I was waiting in the crowd.   It moved, with Moloch gyrations, threatening to absorb the square and the city. It heaved and then withdrew; expanded and then contracted, as if to harden its resolve. Protuberances emerged from its ranks in the shape of small gangs of boys, intent to injure an officer or political man who was not there, but the Moloch's expansions were never prelude to a monstrous uproar and the boy's quickly returned to the ranks; bitter for their first betrayal, as if they'd seen a film icon passed out drunk in his own waste.

The Moloch was never anything more than the paper mache dragon's of the Chinese New Year and its threats to absorb the city nothing more than the expansion and contraction of a sleeping malcontent. The city's forefathers, it seems, had built the square especially for these asthmatic fits.   However, inside this paper mache dragon, huddled between the toilet paper role teeth and the rump, hid the manager; operating the bowels of the beast.

I saw him there. I saw him when he raised the beast above his head and gestured with both hands high in the sky towards the hillside with contempt, as his lips kept time with the others and he counted out his rhythm. One, two, one, two, and through and through. He pushed his tiny Moloch further into the heavens and, as he was taller than the chinamen, the tiny Moloch seemed as a cat arching its back in vague posture-the arch of an animal startled, frightened, and at once on the attack.

And he saw me.

And it all seemed so incongruous.

I wonder how many were there. How many managers? How many card carrying white-collar sympathizers? How many vegetarians in patent leather shoes? How many men playing a boy's game?

The manager is a man. I know this. I have seen him beat the homeless in silence; men don't speak. Of course, the manager does not speak for pride, but such is the case for every man.

He is a man and though masked in the street guerilla's clothes he was sure to set down his tiny Moloch before the crowd dispersed. He exited through the crowd, circumnavigated the city and returned to the hills where his wife and children were waiting on the hillside watching the spectacle below. They had a picnic, and a lovely view.

The deli manager played with his children and from the vantage point on high he educated his son; his son who calls him father. He told him of the secret workings of the State and of the precious rights to assemble and the glorious freedoms that keep the Moloch in the square and the civil man duplicitous. And from his pocket he pulled one of the toilet paper roll teeth of his tiny Moloch and handed it to his boy, and the boy then and there knew, as he was finally entrusted with the common knowledge secret.

• • • • •

But I have no such lessons for my boy.

My boy, raised by my sister, will inherit my pamphlets, but nothing of substance. He will inherit the ideology of the Movement and the songs of the castratos and soon enough, around the time of his first ignoble act, he will desert my sister and inherit my empty stomach.

The manager is standing over my shoulder. He wants to ask if I was sleeping, but the "s" of sleeping is too threatening and besides he knows I have pulled up the skirt of the Moloch and seen what a whore she is. He grows red like the plantation boss caught by his wife with the house slave, as the slave always had something exotic she couldn't give.

Yes, the Moloch's no bride for my boy. And what is left, then? The kitchen?

No.

I'd rather...

The steam of the kitchen is a sauna and I cannot breathe. The windows won't open. There is no ventilation and I wonder even if the kitchen's doors will open the "right way" or if the manager has other designs and I feel behind me, growing in the distance, the dull deafening stampede of protestors and workers who I fear only want to pin me to the door that only pulls open.

I am panicking and I cannot stop.

I am asphyxiating in the kitchen where I am a short order cook and dishwasher.

I look to the door and through its window; through the haze of the collected steam; I see on the other side the round, baldhead of the manager and I know he is holding the door shut.

"A day of women, is it?"

The steam fills my lungs and nostrils, like the sensation of riding in the exposed bed of a truck, and I cannot breathe. I am wrenching and struggling, all the while trying to temper my anxiety, as this must be an anxiety attack.

The steam tastes like a plastic bag drawn tight.

I want to break the window, but I cannot afford the repairs. I want to breathe air and not the soapy water of the dishwasher that burns my hands when I show initiative and am too early to open it. I want to break the window in the door where the manager's head bobs, well at ease, content to drown his dishwasher who saw too much. I want to drown him and if I cannot I want my son to know his name; I want my son to murder him, but I've only a nephew and last night I left him alone in the night that was alive.

I want the manager to open the door, and he does.

He opens the door; walks to the window; turns the handle and pushes it wide open where the steam escapes into the sunlight. He scolds me for not having done so earlier.

I thank him and apologize.

I apologize for wanting to have drowned him and he asks me to leave, but he does not say please, as the "s" is a difficult letter to pronounce, and he has his pride.

He has my pride.

Chapter 6

Yes, I left the boy alone. She doesn't understand. From the day she's taken him she has never understood, and here I know he is more my own, though she is the boy's mother. He is never alone. He is always in the company of himself and in himself he finds a black noise; a sound vacuum.

The boy finds in himself everything his "uncle" finds.

You read it on his face.

Expressions are words and, though his face wears nothing save the stage mask of a stoic player, he communicates.

And I remember the young protestor and his unintelligible rage and I see the boy for the first time and he frightens me. The warn edge of his plastic cereal cup looks now as violent piece of expressionist art, and for its primitive and Klee-like juvenility it is communicating painfully.

I see the boy for the first time and he is tortured.

He is tortured and mad and in the mirror on my sister's vanity, I see myself as a slow drip water torture. I have been his whole life. He has always turned to me and I have always played on his forehead with a steady and maddening consistency, like the dripping of a faucet, seemingly inconsequential and dismissed, though every grand canyon was carved by raindrops, like a faucet.

He only needed time.

I know I should take him in my arms, perhaps comb his hair or comment on how smart he looks, but with raindrops, even if from the faucet...

...hanging over my head, inside my brain, is a pre-seizure cloud and I cannot feel more than the burden to escape the burden.

I leave before I am asked.

It is late afternoon and the sun is dragging long shadows along the street, as I am dragging my broken leg. The horizon, barely visible through the obstructions of the buildings, forms the sun's hips and the shadows, bringing with them night and the summer stars, look very much like the reaching fingers of a man on all fours; dragging himself across the earth. As the night reappears always, the man never rests and I am certain this thought is ugly and sad, but I cannot feel it.

I am as numb as the sole of my foot, lined with blackened toes.

It is comical that my eyes still work, though before I know I could feel the breeze in them. This street I am on was fantastical; I saw visions even when I closed my eyes. The starry nights of Van Gogh haunted my imagination here and every window well lit until the early hours, in particular those windows half-drawn, played on my thoughts.

These were the homes of liaisons between youthful piano instructors and their eager pupils, as equally apt. They were the resting place of lovers tender midnight kisses and the violent embrace of true love; fidelity was born and kept behind these shades that now are gathering dust as the televisions blare in the background and burn the silence from the mind; they burn the canvas from the mind; there is nowhere left to paint and it was not the televisions doing.

Passionate escapades have played against the backdrop of the most trivial American invention. I cannot tell at what point in time the world fell; hidden behind the backdrop of the stage; oppressively two dimensional, however well painted.

The only thing that reminds me my leg is broken is the pulse of blood that dully circulates through my veins and this dirty cast, but the leg is broken and I wish this fact alone could inform my thoughts.

I want to know that I am broken.

I am absurd.

I am always apologetic.

I will take the pain of the fractured bones; the feeble walk; to know that I am broken. But now...I cannot say I would take this gladly, but I will certainly take it.

In the poorly lit street I read the graffiti of the Movement. It occupies walls long since fallen into disrepair, alongside slogans for the local sports club and the bitch who whored herself behind some young man's back or perhaps never reciprocated. I squint to read her name, but the spray paint in illegible; the boy was rushed, or too blinded by betrayal; his craftsmanship suffered, but in this hour, on this street that was once fantastical I do not condemn the messenger anymore for the broken bottle he has flung to the sea's mercy and the water logged now unintelligible letter.

The pollution of the motorcars and scooters wafts through the city on these warm summer nights. For the generation who have never known the clear air of myth; it is carcinogenic and familiar; it reminds me of a woman's body, but I carry the comparison no farther.

I navigate the steady stream of motor scooters that have turned the corner and are heading towards me. They are group of twenty something men. Not a few are missing the large windshields on the front of their scooters; broken either by a flying rock kicked up from the rear tire of a passing truck or automobile, or maybe even another rival group of scooters. The design of the scooters, low riding and the distinct dip of its frame lends itself to the dress of a woman; a woman need not struggle with a skirt's hem, and for the first time, because I am alone, the motor scooter seems to me emasculating.

The motor scooter is emasculating, as are the well-coifed hairdos of each man/boy that rides by. They are meticulous about their appearance and finely tanned even in the winter months. We are a city of models; all on the cover of our own little vogue; all walking the catwalk for the paparazzi below, but here the paparazzi are on stage and no one is admiring no one.

The city is a beautiful woman alone in a restaurant without a man in sight. She is a wealthy man's art collection without an exhibition; she is alone and unappreciated and the boys are flying by like queens wanting to repair their windshields because they miss their reflections. If there are women among them, they are no more than bracelets or a well-placed earring stud or scrotum ring.

It all passes.

A light is on a few blocks down. I see it; across the street from the tourist office lined with several flags I have never taken the time to recognize. I am alone again in the street and the prospect of something fantastic demands I walk the short distance. It is the prospect and not the flame.

I am a blind moth drawn to the stadium's lighting not by the brilliance of the mega watt bulb, but the memory that something as brilliant as the sun ever existed, and I wish my heart had a memory, but it is like a stretch of beach, where lovers together write their vows and return separately to find that the sea has long since washed them away, but their minds cannot forget.

The mind is a burdensome disease. It remembers only enough to torment the empty nights, lying in bed alone, smelling the sweat of a long gone love on fresh sheets; (she smelled so much more wonderful), but all that is left is an empty stretch of beach and the hotel smell of any washed set of linens.

I arrive beneath the window, my mind drunk, laden in discontent. The source of the light is a tiny second hand lamp, with a burgundy shade that paints the wall behind it with a splash of like color. The window is framed by a light drapery that seems forever teased by the breeze; it floats like a vaporous spectre. Ornate metal bars secure whoever is inside, as they secure the van Gogh print hanging from the farthest wall; it is the famous café scene.

I am struggling.

The pre-seizure cloud still hangs menacingly over my head.

I am not trying to communicate; I am trying to make something.

Ambulances speed behind me; the police as well. An old man is walking his dog and old posters are rotting from off the lampposts.

This city is a consumer; blistering her feet inside the latest fashion; sweating profusely inside a too thick summer coat; clogging her pores under layer upon layer of non-comodogenic make-up that, though removed at night, is never removed and she knows this when she wakes in the morning to a filthy pillow case and the running mascara for the tears she cried in her sleep.

The city is a consumer, and my imagination disappears when the lights are off and I cannot see. I do not want the burgundy shade to stop casting light, to stop painting the wall. I do not want it to stop dreaming for me.

My heart has no memory and the palette of my mind can only faintly recreate the splash of color that is youthful infatuation; fondness. The city and I are a kicked dog dreaming in black and white, buying in color.

The lights are off.

Someone turned the lights off.

From down the street I hear a television. It is a commercial for a product I have never tried.

The television is turned off. The street is quiet. The man and his dog are gone and I am alone in the summer.

Inside the window, where the burgundy shade is dark, I hear running water. And through the intricate metal work of the windows bars, in the partition between main room to a back kitchen perhaps, I see the hurried outline of a woman in robe. She is drawing a bath in the dark, and I want nothing more than to be there beside her, huddled between the toilet and the basin, listening to the water give way under and around her form, and I think to myself that candles would be lovely.

Chapter 7

I stand outside this window a long time. I am waiting for something. I am listening to the quiet street, the running water, the colorful play in my mind of thoughts I cannot imagine. When the water stops and the quiet is again interrupted by the sirens and the boys on scooters I will have nothing left of this night; only the imprint, like a fossil, of a moment that was once and once breathed with life.

I want to hold this. I want to hold her, to never let go and to never be let go. I want the impossible satiation and the hunger hope feeds on. I want the burgundy lampshade to light up this room one more time and bathe me in potential forever and a day.

I want salvation in this city, in this politburo city, where religion and faith are the hushed dirty words, whispered in back alleys under the breath of white pill popping ravers losing the memory disease and experiencing ecstasy. They are losing their memory and the remembrance of the white pills failure to obliterate. They will take more and more, dancing in the primitive heat of their amnesiac minds, fighting the encroaching dawn and the sober thoughts where past is recollected and they are still too heavy and they've still birthing hips.

They all look to me like the priests of the church, and their church, their monastery, is the converted underground furnished with disco ball, strobe lights, and transubstantiation; I know the boys who enter and the women who leave are of the same bread the techno devoured; nothing changes; the Church knows everything except me.

It is raining, and I am convulsing in seizure. I do not want to swallow my tongue and my words and my thoughts for the Church, the techno, the castratos and their bracelets; I only want to stand again and walk. And I want this because I am paralyzed and soiling myself in a pile by the road.

I will sleep. I do not have a choice. The pre-seizure cloud has erupted. I am drenched in urine and the storm of thoughts and rain. The curb I am sleeping in is funneling the raw sewage across my body. Hamburger wrappers collect at my feet, occasionally breaking free to cover my face and threaten suffocation, but they are soon carried away either by the wind or the river developing in the sides of the road.

I can think nothing of this; I am unconscious.

The world carries on without my consent.

I wake to the proddings of a police officer.

I am slurring like a drunk.

He pulls me from the sewage.

He pulls me from the sewage.

He pulls me from the sewage...

With principle I spit into his face; his face with the fresh scar across its forehead; his face that knows very well the rules of the game. And like the exceptional sparring partner I took him for, he beats me severely.

I am unconscious again and wake to a loss of memory; the beating escapes me and I laugh at this because I won. I laugh because I reached ecstasy. I laugh because the police officer in shining uniform beat a lady.

This makes me want to giggle, and I do careful to cover my mouth with my hand so as to prevent a cultural blunder or worse even, a fauz pas. I cover my face like a polite Japanese girl, with the snobbish airs of a Parisian lady, with the feigned sensibility of a Bedouin woman already covered from head to toe; the action is unnecessary. There is no one around who would dare question that I am a right proper lady.

The only ones now around are the early morning garbage collectors.

I recognize one. He is my comrade. Or rather he was my comrade. I am tempted to explain away my bruises and cuts with the truth, but I've no interest; the words are not my own; the intentions are not my own. I would only be a well-rehearsed actor declaiming into the black void of the audience, declaiming to another actor concentrating on his own pre-scripted rejoinder, declaiming and not communicating anything other than a commitment to the director's pre-determined objectives and tactics. It is a strange role and one I was born to play, but I've lost interest and would much prefer to work as a stage hand in the wings, forgetting his queue, or to play this role deaf, blind, and mute with the manager's speech impediment lisping my way through the most weighty and significant lines of the piece.

I am a subversive.

"We're meeting tonight."

"I'm not well."

"Are you a peeping tom?"

"Yes, but I want to be more."

"More?"

"I want to imagine stories for them."

"You're a pornographer."

"Now I am. I want to be more. I want to make something"

"Come to the meeting. We are making something."

"Yes."

I hope I am lying. I want desperately to not be there. They are making nothing. They make nothing; they carry only the current of history to its conclusion; the current is not there's, and history is very old.

She is the first pope sealed in a glass box delivered to the feet of the returned Christ; she never left the lord's side and their individual efforts could never undermine this current.

The Movement is made of journeymen and apprentices, but the masters are all in prisons, and for this they are all insignificant; martyrdom was invented for history and the inconsequential; a pacifier for a child who must teethe or a gold medal awarded after forfeiture. We shout their names, but that is all.

I want desperately to not be there. Already I see my hand shattering the glass casket of the pope before the final hands of the Movement's tradesmen have delivered it to an appreciative yet expectant messiah. If only the garbage collector knew that now.

As it is, he does not know.

I am working in the belly of the Moloch in the square; I feel as though I've a Billy club in hand.

I want this.

I will make the only grab at potency I can, however weakened, frail, and horrifically desperate. I will abduct the child from the park for my barren womb and raise myself into a man. And I will damn the comrades and the Movement and the current of history for a single stone to negotiate the barrel of a tank and win me an inch, one goddamn inch, of occupied territory. I am in the square attacking on all fronts, my own city, my own nation; my own patriot.

I will be there.

Now though, I am badly beaten and the cast on my leg has not faired well in the road's drainage. My comrade leaves, hugging tightly to the rear of the garbage truck, reeking of diapers and everything fit for compost. I watch him leave with foreign eyes; the eyes of a man strange to his environment and growing familiar to himself; his character seemingly articulated in contrast to what he is not; the brilliance of his culture, in his mind, shining in the chiaroscuro of encounters with natives.

I want to run after the Garbage Collector, shouting, "Comrade! Comrade!" as if we were a classic American western. I never want him to leave my sight, to breach the horizon and sink beneath the crest of earth. I want him to stay forever here. I want him to identify me. As what he is, I am not, and without him I cannot tell my boy how to be. And I think that perhaps this is why I will be there tonight. Why I will gather in a circle in a café, imbibing drinks, rhetoric, and fears dressed in good intentions.

I am not them. I am not their comrade.

I am nothing less than a subversive and here, perhaps, is the bulb where everything of substance blooms. The roots that grow, like the willow, and drink directly from the river's banks; I am not waiting for the rain, the State's handouts, the audience's applause. I am digging, like a mole, digging incessantly. And though I am blind and the earth's vermin parasite, I am buried alive and moving.

I have not needed anything else.

I am buried alive and moving, and soon I will negotiate the meetings of the Movement, playing loch and levy. I will raise their ambitions and redirect their current until flatly it lands on the delicate sarcophagus of an embalmed pope and their own aspirations. And they will curse me Judas and more, as Judas himself never rolled the tide of history into an ebb and drowned the Christ among the clams. And I do so for the self I cannot realize except in conflict.

I am fighting the stasis of the Movement. I am fighting the utopia that marries man to woman and excises the lust. I am struggling against the absurdity of falling pleasantly asleep and ever wishing to wake, as exhaustion is the fuel of dreams and unfulfillment the inspiration to rise. Always.

The street is swimming in commuters. The vendors are opening shop and muffins are being sold to combat constipation and coffee to combat constipation. And I feel violently derisive and sanctioned by life to blaspheme and question why everyone is so tight assed and whoever got it into their head that the worker was noble and the clever wicked.

I am straggling home. My leg is rubbing against my cast and the friction burns my toes to sensation; I am feeling the cobblestones through my shoes.

I walk into the square that leads to the boy and my sister's apartment. The café waitress is smoking on her morning break. Her figure is awash in the morning light, unobstructed, as the sun has risen high. She bats the steady stream of smoke around her as a kitten, laxadasilly reclining in the sunlight from a window, playing with a dangling window treatment. Her form is supine in her chair; she owns herself wholly and I see this.

Her dark hair billows without coarseness.

Her breasts are full and, though she is seated, her hips are a heavenly proportion; my mind is wrapped around them and my burdened head is resting on her chest. I want to taste her skin, the salt off her immaculate complexion made all the more so for every imperfection placed their by a deft craftsman; they signal her materiality; they say she is real; she can be touched.

But I reek of a man absolved in his own fluids. I head home and shower. I am careful not to make a disturbance, but there is no one home to disturb; my sister is at work. Though the entire exercise takes little more than a few minutes, it feels like an eternity as I barge through the apartment's rusted screen door and maneuver my way with formula1 precision to the café and the waitress.

And now, buried alive, breathing through every pore of my body, each of my hairs feeling my way through a tunnel of my own design; I order espresso and situate myself without conscious design of being conspicuous, except to the waitress. I am seated near the entrance to the kitchen where she repeatedly passes by carrying dirty trays of plates and utensils or overpriced sandwiches. Her smell mixes with every meal and I am pleased that after two or three passes by I can distinguish her own body's fragrance. It is lovely. Not in the least like a fruit or floral smell, but rather the smell of her; her body; the body she will wash off after work self-consciously; the body she hides under overpriced perfumes and scented bath bars purchased in packages with exfoliating sponges. I smell her and nothing she can say will equal this bliss, and the injustice of this truth does not faze me anymore and I feel, perhaps, as an animal.

I smell her and I respect her and the ideologies she clings to, as the ideologies of all men and women, are of little consequence; they are the ridiculous trappings of a ridiculous and arrogant humanity. A worldview is the pinpoint in a person's life where their unifying truth is revealed to be hidden under the point of a pin.

I want to own her and not her education. I want the woman before the literacy, as I wanted myself before the Movement. I want to have her served to me, as the Dutch would serve tulip bulbs. I want her innate, primitive, verve before the floral shop raped her in arrangement; before she was preened and proper. I want her to pass by and I want to smell the shit of the fertilizer still clinging to her clothes and I want her in my bed.

I want to own her. Not as a man owns property, or with the communal understanding of the Movement; I want to own her as a man wants to own experience, as he could never own anything, save in dreams. I want to be diffused through her, floating in an ether. I want to possess her. I want her to possess me, and I want fully an understanding.

I tell her we're meeting here tonight.

The cafes name is Montaigne's backroom.

I wonder of the deli manager will be here. No matter, really; I will be as duplicitous for the both of us. In fact, I fully intend to wear many faces; encompassing all perspectives; making mad calculated stabs at consolidation and victory.

She asks about the Party's aim. She asks why.

I satisfy her curiosity with the Party line, knowing how easily it is deconstructed. One day or night I will tell her the truth. As is the case with men, you cannot trust women, but you can trust a woman. After a man and woman's spirits are wed, in that moment when the surge of their sexes bleeds into a deluge a man and a woman can rule circumstance with an obstinate wisdom; even in abject poverty.

She says she will be there, though I never asked. I would never ask her that, and I am furious. She turns around with the check in hand and tends to the other customers.

The walk home to the apartment is marred by trivial disturbances amplified in the light of the waitress' revelation. Boys on bicycles in the way, contemptuous faces of pedestrians not directed towards me, the white gloved police officer directing traffic and preventing the accidents I desperately want to see; all conspire to frustrate my perfect evening; the evening of my ascension; the evening I embark on an expedition, as parasite, to the center of the earth.

She will be there.

She will be there and she will certainly witness the mole in leg cast, scurrying among the Movement's ranks, barking dissent and exuding subversion, as a rodent.

She will be there at the meeting and I must convert her because I cannot lie to her, and now she is the only one with that distinction. I can lie to the comrades. I can lie to the deli manager with his Moloch draped across his shoulders.

I walk up the stairs to the apartment, enter and find another soul I had not thought to confront with the truth. My boy is sitting in front of a television. The image is scrambled, but the sound is clear like a radio if you sit close enough.

I cannot lie to the boy and am grateful he does not speak or ask questions.

The television show is recognizable through the snow of the screen. The plot is predictable. It is the type of show watched only to be ridiculed and I hang my heart in shame that my life to date has only amounted in the consumption of popular culture. The well-timed tears of my sister collected in her tissue, as she sits on the couch, resemble in no small way blood clots coughed into a turn of the century consumptive's handkerchief; they fall as scripted as the dialogue. She is rotting from the inside and my boy is raving outside the disco.

I can take no more and, without hesitation, I turn the television off.

My sister rises from her seat in a blind fury and quickly turns the television back on. She waits a few moments for the image to reappear, adjusting the antennas and devoting not a little time to the exercise; all for the perfect show; balance of sound and image; a mind numbing complete work of art.

She returns to the couch her eyes glaringly fixed on me, I know, as I look outside the window and the crackle of the television fills the room; I see her reflection in the film across the pane.

And then it dies.

I turn around.

The boy is standing in front of the screen. His plastic cup of cereal is lying beside him and he is supporting his frame on the on/off switch of the box.

Chapter 8

The meeting is a loud affair. Most conversation is unrelated to the topics at hand. The Movement is mostly made of artists and musicians; men and women of the pass the buck philosophy; co-opting the message for the medium and the un-esteemed praise of the crypto-fascist art critics and connoisseurs who endow their work.

For those rare few who truly believe and engage their entire being in the Movement; they do not exist. Those who approximate this type more closely resemble the deli manger for his obsessive neuroses; they do not sleep well; they do not eat well and they are more like the prison bitch taking It as this is all the ward has to offer. They are taking it and now, today, I understand them less and feel a greater kinship to the hypocrites in dreadlocks and would feel even more so would they confide in me, but such alliances are self-defeating; we all must maintain our outward appearances.

The waitress is not here yet and I am hopeful that she will not show. The meeting seems more and more like a mountain range that I am surveying, looking for my peak where I will summit.

The garbage collector calls the meeting to order. He is unshaved and still smells of the truck. He will smell of the truck always however far he climbs in the Party's ranks. He is weighted down by his identification with the Movement and its ideology. It is like an unnecessary provision, as easily abandoned at the base of the mountain, but kept in good faith, as earlier expeditions used as much, however unsuccessful.

Lord knows he, as well, wants to be at the top.

No, the garbage collector is a neurotic, like so many. He is not important and the rowdiness of those called to order demonstrates this. He is a brochure; a pamphlet; a book as long as its liner notes; he is read before he opens his mouth, and this lends itself to dissent.

The Movement, like the ravers' club, is a new church, where amen is heard in the parishioners' dissension; it is the rule and not the exception. The artists, bohemians, and open-minded are blatant saboteurs, frustrating the Movement, which in and of itself is not so vulgar, as the script demands the Movement's impotence, but the tactlessness is inexcusable; it is the mark of a poor performer; the noticeable misappropriation of the Movements pseudo-momentum; they want the Movement to speak for them foolishly believing their human experience could ever be addressed in a single manifesto and nurtured to fruition.

The Bohemians are players improvising and they have no talent for it.

I am tempted to shout the dissenters down; to remonstrate them for their ignorance. They are standing in the ocean, their arms held before them, commanding the waves to stop their breaking.

It is not enough to dissent; it reveals a slow intellect. It reveals an actual belief in the righteousness and power of the Movement. Nothing will come of this. The Movement is impotent. If the players' base appetites are ever to be addressed the Movement's impotence must be accounted for. Ideologies are the runt of humanity's litter; borne to be abused and to lend substance and majesty to those who topple them. Christ is magnificent for the plight of the Jews, for the plight of his own people.

The players need to commit to their direction and wait in their dressing rooms after the performance. I am asking for a reformation; these "amens" delay production. An actor is only an actor so long as he is on stage.

The waitress is here.

She is dressed in the clothes she wore this morning.

She sits beside the garbage collector.

The fog is lifted and I find the peak, once hidden. He invited her and I will ruin him.

The exercise of summitting is to bring yourself to the grandeur of the mountain and to place it firmly beneath your feet. Until she arrived, before the clouds that accumulate at the base of massive formations had dissipated, I did not see his magnificence, but now; now it is abundantly clear.

His ruin is my Everest. And the Movement is a river demanding a Herculean effort to redirect; I am cleaning stables; nothing more, really. The ruin of a man, the heart of a woman, the climbing of a mountain; it is all cleaning stables.

I smile to myself because here the ground is won and the myths, like clean air, cannot be erased from the public's consciousness. Still inside, I recognize it will not be a favorable light they paint me with in frescoes, but favorable lighting is the domain of the actor and here; I am in the wings working the curtains, and missing queues.

"You're awfully quiet. Don't you say anything in meetings?"

"Are you listening?"

"Yes."

"Is anyone saying anything?"

She thinks politely for a moment and then smiles the conspirator's smile.

Yes, one day or night I will tell her.

The garbage collector is struggling to be heard. I wonder if it is necessary to ruin him, as motions are made already in side conversations to remove him. These motions will never pass or ever be voiced for that matter; he is the opposition's source of contempt. What will they hate without him; without him to subvert the Movement and its possibilities the players will have to own their failures. For them it best that he stands there a blubbering idiot; an effigy of their shortcomings that they burn in gossip.

If only she did not look at this burning Guy Fawkes.

I will tell her soon. I will tell her that her garbage collector presides over a dying Moloch; it is suffering from a parasite, burrowing through its blood stream; irritating the lining of its veins. It is succumbing to a river blindness brought in the labor of a once dishwasher now stable boy. In its blindness, I will tell her...the Moloch will forget convention and raise itself to the surrounding hills, and the picnickers will pull from their baskets Billy clubs to beat it down and dead and the city will know Judas, hurling stones like David, felling goliath in Abraham.

Chapter 9

The meeting ends. The bohemians file through the door with the airs of men and women exiting a church, having performed their service; having won the privilege to identify themselves as Christians; as political. They will fuck tonight, their bodies channeling, as some deranged mediums, the sexual potency of the Movement. It will escape in their sweat and in their voices. Mistakenly they will ride the Party platform to orgasm; shouting its name and making no apologies. And as the buck their partner, the opposition will topple below their gyrations and in their minds, as they lie exhausted, piled on one another; they will gaze into their reflections, as they always keep a mirror beside the bed, and they will see conquistadors. They will smell virility and they will not change their sheets.

And she is hand in hand with the garbage collector.

She is walking away. She is turning a few paces from the door and waving good-bye. And he is kissing her and mounting her in his thoughts, and his thoughts are cluttered with the Party mantra; he does not think of her.

Not as I think of her.

Not with my selfishness.

Love admits cruelty; it must.

The garbage collector knows only neurotic compassion. He is wringing his hands, stepping over cracks, exchanging tofu recipes, and committing Janist suicide. He is married to the Party.

She is not his inspiration, as he is not a true artist himself, but moreover because she is his medium; she is his sculptor's clay; the painter's oils and canvas; the musician's strings and horns and piles of compositions scattered across the floor; she is his sublimation. He is fucking her; looking at his reflection and fucking her in the name of the Movement, and she is receiving like a downtrodden mass. In his garbage collector's eyes she is receiving, like the opposition and in his climax, in his summit; he rapes me.

She passes through the door and out of sight and in this I am dragged into a dark alley and violated by her garbage collector. I want to scream; the screams of young woman; the screams of a girl not yet acquainted with the notion of honor; who having danced the night with her first true love at a chaperoned function would scream; in tears and smothered wailing, pleading not for her father or her family, but the young man, dew-eyed around a punch bowl who will never be her first; she will never have a first.

And it is the Movement that made this impure sex; this impure love; the rape and the "day after boy" that sees a woman where yesterday stood a young girl.

Love admits cruelty, but not deceit, and his is a bed of lies, as I know he comes with his face in the pillow, burying his Party loyalties for the next lay.

The evening is warm. The sky is clear, and the stars in this pitch-black canopy are as flat as paper.

There is a vendor on the corner. He is open later than most, selling newspapers and magazines; all filled with obsolete information. They are useless. I walk over to him and place my hand on the Party's paper. He is a foreigner. In the corner of his mobile shack his grandson sits, tended to by his mother. They are oblivious to me; she is feeding him and talking to him. The old vendor quotes me the papers price and then turns to the woman and demands that she stop speaking their language to the family's first native born.

The boy repeats the woman's sentence fragments with the same mispronunciations that will plague him and reaffirm his own alienation when he is enrolled in the city's schools; he will always feel a foreigner even after he is corrected his speech. He will speak with the mastered annunciation of a television broadcaster. His skilled assimilation will emphasize his homelessness.

The vendor asks if I am going to buy the paper.

I say no and walk away with it in hand.

He does not run after me; the paper is not worth the aggravation.

I smile; a pathetic victory; a display of painful irony; his grandson will join the Movement. He is already being raised a Bedouin without a home and the city will botch his circumcision well enough. And the paper in my hand...I am the homely sister raiding the princes' wardrobe.

Beneath a lamppost's light I read an article by the garbage collector. Though he is in direct contact with the bohemian players and artists, the students who run the press do not trust his ability to communicate in print; his article is printed on the third page. It is of nothing consequential. The students are right; he is an idiot.

The students belong to a distinct branch of the Movement with a steady rotating membership of three to four years; five for the heavy pot smokers. They are as committed to the cause so long as their job is academics and sporting the fashionable attire of the Movement doesn't conflict with their employment in the consulting business they take under pressure from their families.

In demonstrations they hang from the radio's truck and dance bacchanalian behind the banners; drinking and smoking. Their presence is the reason the city provides street sweepers and large cleaning trucks. The trucks follow the rally directly behind the armored police, police vans, and ambulances. The street sweepers seem almost to not just erase the refuse that lingers, testament to the demonstrations presence, but also its memory. When the tourists develop their film back in Florida or Sheffield they will remember the rally, but only vaguely and the pictures will look more to them like a Berlin love parade.

The tourists were caught unawares and could not focus their cameras to catch the banners message, but they saw the students; they saw the city's future consultants sewing oats under the same flag.

I throw the paper into the garbage.

Coming directly towards me is the old man I saw the night before. He is haggard looking up close and his dog moves with arthritic care and the stumble of a lush. The old man is disoriented; he is talking to himself, running his own rheumatic fingers along his dry, chapped bottom lip.

"It was around here somewhere."

"What was?"

"It was around here somewhere."

"What was old man?"

The man asks his dog if he remembers.

"Why are you asking the dog?"

"Because he lives there too."

The man's rosacea gives him the appearance of a healthy glow for which there is no real reason; he is not healthy. His mind is failing and he is lost.

"What is your name?"

He tells me his name and I recognize him as the grandfather of a childhood friend. The friend no longer lives there. She has done well for herself and lives in the country.

"I'm taking you home."

"Yes? We're going home, boy."

The walk is relatively short and it seems as though the old man has been out for some time; a few hours, perhaps.

Inside his apartment, where he now lives alone, he offers me tea and something to eat. I decline and say I have to go. On the way out I notice that his wall is strewn with the memorabilia of a Party man.

"Are you a member?"

I say nothing and he continues.

"I knew you were a Party man! You have the Party spirit."

"How's that?"

And through the warm eyes of the hopelessly naïve and the enviably deluded he says, "because you brought me home."

And before I exit into the night as flat as paper where newspapers are stolen because love is unrequited I turn and ask, "Since when is compassion an ideology, old man?"

And the blasphemy cleanses the soul.

Chapter 10

He spoke.

The boy spoke.

When I was away at the meeting.

His "mother" was cleaning the carrots for dinner and he was in his high chair. She'd left the window open as the night was hot and the air conditioner and ceiling fan are both broken down.

"One of the cats jumped onto the ledge."

"Was she pregnant?"

"I couldn't tell."

"And that's when he said-"

"That's when I thought I heard him say "cat.""

"It wasn't cat."

"No, he said it again-"

"And he was saying-"

"He was saying, "bad.""

I remember a girl from Madrid.

She was a painter; a great fan of Lichtenstein and Warhol; the American classic few Americans have an appetite for. In her run down apartment in the Turkish part of town, where she would chain smoke joints and listen to movie soundtracks to movies she had never seen, she tried explaining to me once the act of seeing, and I tried to bed her with the manifesto propped as a pillow.

"Before you open your eyes," she said, my eyes stinging under a second hand high, "you open your heart; the world's a Rorschach test."

The world's a Rorschach test, and I don't know if the boy and I have failed.

We have both begun our maturation. Mine is, of course, late, but the boy's, in the spring of his life; I see a harvest in the fall and wonder what fruits will be gathered and what grains will be reaped. His hand is to the soil, dispersing unknown seeds that will absorb from the soil all there is to offer; all its nutrients and moisture, and all its poisons. Unknown seeds, as I do not know the depths that the anchor of his first word has plunged.

He has identified a cat, and like the first man he knows, instinctually, that the plants and animals are his. As I know they are mine, as they are every man's to dismiss or bring close to the bosom.

He is informing his world, and I do not yet know the magnitude of his words. I do not know the significance of "bad" and the incommunicable rage or sense of justice that resounds inside his tiny frame that still struggles to walk. And when he runs he will run, and I am terrified his labor will amount to little more than a Sisyphean exercise and his legs will carry him little further than to the base of the hills, where the rock of his activity will drag him once again into the fray of the masses and the carnival of the square, and he will be made a fool mistaken for a king...

... and perhaps I see my own failures.

He has chosen a word.

The boy has a voice.

And right or wrong and the absurd game mean nothing to a man and his garden with a single red youthful rose. And I know that I will preen either the thorn or the bloom to perfection.

He is my son.

He is my son, and I tell him this. I do not know if he understands or much cares. He stares at me with the look of a man awaking from a long coma and I hope that this is the case. I want very much for him to see his father ascend to the pinnacle of this city's heights even if I must open the earth to swallow her. I want this and I want him to be there if only that I might survey the next valley and offer it as my passing gift and my final word and my only wisdom that yes, Alexander, there is more to conquer.

"Alexander, there's more."

He smiles a knowing smile; the smile of the youth who loses his wisdom in university and then regains it in the real world. He smiles, as if to say, it has always been this way, welcome home.

And for the first time I pull the boy with affection on to my knee and hold him in the cradle of my arms, whispering the devotion in my heart and of the mountains and rivers and even stray cats made for him and I.

My sister is crying in the kitchen and the world is a different place in an apartment where the ceiling fan does not work and the air conditioner will never work again.

PART 2

Chapter 1

He asks where I am living. I say with my sister and my son. He lets me inside. He lets me inside because I am not homeless and I remember the papier-mache dragon and his humiliation and release in the bowels of the beast.

"You want to drown me."

Yes, I do.

"No."

"Why are you here? Do you have pictures?"

No, of course not.

"Yes."

"How much?"

He is crying. The deli manager is crying, like a closeted celebrity husband outed in a supermarket tabloid. I give him a second to compose himself and feel relieved at the prospect. His wife will no doubt forgive him for the children's sake and the children will not appreciate the shame until they are older and can fall back on it in session; he will be the source of their own inconsistent behavior contrary to everything they "know" and "have been taught."

Children will always neglect what they have truly been taught about the world. Here is your lesson, sir- Movements as governments live and die by the charisma of the Big men; the Movement never looks as promising and on the move as it does when in the arms of a strapping college boy. Your son, the one educated on the hill, does not appreciate that the method to the madness is the madness and that Caesar lost his crown long before he was butchered and that his father is, as the Bedouins a screaming queen.

None the less, "nothing really."

I want everything.

"Why are you here?"

I am here as the one man to set you free. I am squeezing your proverbial arm tightly behind your back and wrenching your body forward into contortions that will never be your doing or your fault. I am promising you bliss by holding over your head the promise of public absolution; I am your confessor and the magistrate teasing from you your deepest secret. I am demanding of you your heart's grandest wish. I am demanding that you fulfill your fantasies.

I am making you yourself and giving you the reigns to ride fully in chariot over the backs of saints. I am the serpent in the garden and the messiah at the end of all creation.

"I am a dishwasher in need of a favor."

He collects himself, washes his hands and face, and listens.

On the way out he gathers his Billy club and with the look of a portly teenage boy relegated by a spun bottle to kiss the pretty class president, he shrugs and exits out through the side alley, and I only now register that he never used soap.

Chapter 2

A special meeting is called. I arrive to find everyone reading today the atrocities of last night.

"He was beaten"

"By whom?

"It was with a Billy club"

"Who do you think?"

"The police-"

"Fucking fascists!"

"They found it in his pocket."

"Found what?"

"Do you have a paper?"

"I need one."

"He's a Party member."

"Is that why?"

"An old man walking his dog."

"What's his name?"

"What happened to the dog?"

"What page?"

"Aren't you reading?"

"What page?"

"Front"

"But why?"

"What did they find, it's not in here."

"The story carries over."

"Why do they insist on littering the pages with women in bathing suits; this is not news."

"What did they find?"

"They found flyers; he was putting up flyers."

"They?"

"The police!"

"We're sure."

"Flyers?"

"It doesn't say; wait-here it is-"

And the Movement is solidified and the Movement is waiting for a resolve.

"And the dog? What happened to the dog?"

"You don't want to know."

But they do. They want to know everything, but the truth. They do not want to hear how the deli manager found the old man, late at night, walking with his dog along the same streets I'd found him earlier. They don't want to know anything other than a story of a police officer who's only real crime was not being there when the old man was asked where he lived, and he couldn't answer and he couldn't say he was not at that time and place homeless.

The story they want is the final chapter of a martyr. They want undefiled innocence. They want the officer to be identified in line-up by the festering puncture wounds of a dog's bite. But they will not have an officer served to them, and they will blame the city. They will not have an officer with festering wounds because the dog never moved; he stood there as the deli manager, with Billy club, came down on the old man as if under demonic possession, as if the old man were Job and he was working him over for a denunciation that never came because the deli manager never asked. The old man fell as a regiments flag bearer; ignorant of the colors he was carrying; ignorant of the cause he furthered.

It is almost painfully ironic. The old man and his arthritic dog are dead, and for his

Party loyalty the Party is organizing itself for ruin. And I suppose this is the way for every conflict; a fallen soldier, even if the drummer boy or a molly pitcher, dies for the oppositions cause. It seems a cruel indoctrination. The old man's death is a mythologized martyrdom for the Movement, but he was a soldier in my ranks and I want almost to eulogize him.

And I want to march the deli manager through the streets of Rome, in procession with his captives, with the body of the old man and his dog, sweltering in the summer heat in the same plastic duffel-like body bag. I want to bring him to the forum, through the adorations of the ill-informed populace and I want to murder him. I want to place a laurel around his ears and a sash of sorts across his chest leading to his soft under side and here, as I will bring him to my arms, my dagger will plunge itself deep into his bowels. And his bowels I will operate like a marionette and he will dance and murder for me before I am through and discard him; he is already dead.

He is my puppet. He is my punch. He is as alive as any man dangling beneath the dexterous fingers of another. He is like the cardinals under the pope and the ravers under the d.j. and the d.j. under the ravers' expectations and appetite for drum and bass.

I want to murder a man I have already killed, and this does not seem incongruous to me.

I allow contradictions free reign in myself; in others they are abominable.

And this is a righteous allowance.

Only the arrogant dismiss contradictions. Only the arrogant and proud, who huddle around historical texts and mathematical equations; who peruse each scrap of history for insights into the future; who unify the past and present into a theory for the future; only these men huddled and confined in their ivory tower academic offices, around their historical tea leaves and mathematical crystal balls, are arrogant enough to dismiss contradictions. Only they are arrogant enough to offer the world up to their capacity for deduction. The rest, the saintly, have no such luxury; we play the fools in the square, but we are not the real fools on the throne. We are not the fools who butcher on a hot day in June striking workers, as they are frustrating the workers' revolution; we do not have the foresight.

My subversion is reactionary, but it emerged long before the Movement.

"What do we do?"

The garbage collector is looking for a consensus.

I tell them I need time to think. They send me on my way with consolations, as "I knew the man's granddaughter."

They understand and tell me when the next meeting will be.

"Tomorrow night. Here again."

I leave into the midday haze and the throngs of pedestrians that tire my eyes. They move with such rapidity, from all directions. I cannot focus properly to take them all. I am swimming in their contrasts, their dizzying colors and appearances; I am fighting to maintain my opinion and objectivity; to inform everything I see; to not concede an inch of ground for experience to overwhelm my perception of it; for my heart to be flooded by another's voice and another's ill-formed thoughts; I cannot possess a flawless idea, but I will be damned if I possess another's and betray myself in the process.

The haze intrudes my eyes and renders everything an impressionist painting where the clear delineation of form is obliterated. The foreground blends with the background of everything I see and like a window opening onto a brick wall in a slum this is all I see. With brushstrokes I want to paint the bricks the color of fresh air. I want to breathe.

This is not remorse. I feel no remorse for what the deli manager has done. My eyes are tired. Sleep will make them strong again to see what they want to see and not what they are told.

Chapter 3

The deli manager is washing his hands.

He is trying to wash the blood off them. He should not work so hard. His hands are raw and the blood is his own.

The Billy club, lying in the sink, has been washed so many times the paint is worn off.

"It will splinter."

He doesn't answer.

"They're clean."

"What have I done?"

"You were there. You know better than anyone. Only the old man could know more, but...well, you know more than anyone."

He stops washing his hands and uncharacteristically braces himself on the sinks rim; his arms are shaking. His pathetic lips, formed as a Frenchman's, the lips that betray his lisp before he opens his mouth are fumbling nervously. His upper lip glistens. His face is unshaved. His arms are hairy, masculine, like a Mediterranean's, and he is vomiting.

He is purging himself of every ounce of guilt and every fear of reprisal that will never be fully purged. The days will pass into weeks and months and years. From here on every other thought will be a furtive glimpse over a shoulder for the police not at the door, or a head slung low on the shoulders dragging memories, shameful memories through the conscience.

He is a diseased man, standing apart from the lot of humanity; occupying a space in the cities consciousness without a face.

In the mirror beside his bed, he will see the murderer of the old man and his dog when the Movement and the city see only a uniform that is not real.

"What have I done?"

"You have taken yourself as far as you wanted to go."

"I want to go back. I'm so sorry."

And he is. He is terribly sorry. I would not be surprised if he killed himself.

"Why didn't you do it yourself?"

We are in an empty kitchen. The tap drips at extended intervals. Sunlight broaches the threshold of the open alley door. The air is still; the still air of an empty shed in a too familiar place that promises nothing and makes you want to sleep. It is the feel of expressionless tile or sad wood where unwashed garden tools are kept. It is an old feel and answering this question is laborious.

I will not tell him.

The answer is deeply personal, as it is for every man. The answer is the vulgar thought that I respect the law. The unsavory idea that I am at once complicit in its downfall and in its regrowth. I am severing diseased limbs, that threaten the home during a storm, and the home is mine. I have hired a man to remove the limbs, and to preserve the tree. It is not authority I despise, but my own impotence in the face of authority. The law at my back is a road rising to my feet; it is luminous and breathtaking. The law in my face is a whore.

He asks again, "Why didn't you do it yourself?"

His eyes are the strained red of a man after convulsions. His stubble has specks of puke trapped in it. His fingers are surgical clean with streaks of his blood flowing in the crevices of his knuckles.

And for reasons that escape me, but still I yield, I tell the deli manager. I tell him the truth, as the lying was strenuous.

"I never had pictures of the square and your dancing with the chinamen."

He collapses into a pile on the ground. His stomach bloated in the realization; he is full on himself. He has eaten too much to digest; he will purge again, as he cannot deny that he was the one to beat the old man to death and he cannot deny that his proverbial arm was never truly tied behind his back, contorting his body into the shape needed to wield a Billy club and dent a man's skull and torture an animal mercilessly.

He should have known earlier. I never asked him to torture the dog.

Chapter 4

I do not remember numbness.

I leave the deli manager's kitchen.   I leave him on the floor. I leave him in that State where a man can vomit on himself, soil himself, and not move; fully conscious of one fact and only slightly registering that what is transpiring is odd.

If the deli manager is numb to his environment; he is in a State I cannot remember. It is as difficult to recreate in the mind, as the thrill of a first love; the palette of the mind is missing this color, as well. The mind has little resuscitative powers. It seems capable only of enhancing an experience; of an enlivening an otherwise drab wall with a well-framed picture, but it cannot recreate the foundation. The mind cannot recreate the wall; it cannot recreate love.

Numbness is as love; it is dumb, mute; a drug no junkie can buy; an ailment no pharmacy

can cure. I no longer want to play the kicked
dog, dreaming black and white, purchasing its
world in color, but it does not seem I have a
choice. My mind cannot recreate the despair in
my breast that would cause me to turn around
and empathize with the man I've left in his own
yellow bile.

I pass a used appliance store. The metal
grating is being pulled down, but the televisions
are still on inside. The owner will leave through
a backdoor. On the screens I see the
commercials for the children of the third world.
A rotund white American woman is imploring
me to help her. I have seen the commercial
before and though the sound is off I hear her in
my memory well enough to know a cup of
coffee a day is all it takes.

A cup of coffee a day and every well
thinking man and woman of this city could think
well of themselves legitimately. But most do
not move; only the neurotic; the men and
women racing one another to an ulcer; fearful of
the cloth or their secular humanitarian preachers
they call professor. For the rest, we pass by the
request for the money. We dismiss the children
with the eyes disproportionate to their emaciated
faces. We carry on with our lives and spend
fully 8 times "the price of a cup of coffee" on a
cup of coffee at the nearest espresso chain store.

I cannot remember the deli manager's
numbness; it is his own. Like the experience of
Auschwitz a young writer could never fathom
even with the perfect words. And in this, the
human experience, for its isolation and
loneliness, is a precious one; at least my own

experience; I cannot speak for the deli manager or the old man he murdered.

I trip across a man lying prostrate in the street. Children, his own evidently, are begging him to wake up, but he does not respond. One of the children is seated on a stores single step crying. She is a pretty girl of roughly ten years; she reminds me of the children I have seen in the commercials, though this is not a third world. She is thin and no doubt hungry. Her father has spent the family's money on the great escape.

Her hands are extended and she is begging of me. Change. I reach into my pockets and offer her what little I have. It is all I have. I think nothing of this and give no consideration to my own child at home. She smiles. She smiles; her head slightly tilted; her eyes a genius hazel; her hair a complementary black. She says thank you.

I cannot make sense of the exchange. I allow the inconsistencies to flow through my person and experience, like the irrigation system to a field of maize; I leave it unobstructed. I leave the little girl, as I left the deli manager; I leave them to themselves, but I extended a hand to one.

The method to my life is madness, but I regret nothing and have not betrayed myself in the least. I am smelling the warm airs of the twilight hours and the women, wearing bottles of perfumes, still unable to mask their pheromones. I have not betrayed myself.

The twilight hours are a shifting bouquet; its fragrances changing from the diesel exhaust of the day's trucks that crammed the busy city streets, into the smells of the corner restaurants with open doors and windows; a cornucopia of transient sensations. Nothing is permanent in these hours, like the affections of a young man and the dress of a young woman; they are traded numerous times before the moon gains its place in the sky and the stars are no longer bleached by the sun; the sun obstinate and ever unwilling to relinquish its hold over the day.

This is at once the waning hours and the hours of emergence, and if I read in the course of nature truth I would find my own behavior, my own contradictions, celebrated in the fickle seasons that never consent to remain one, but rather divide into four. And they are four indecisive seasons. I have seen the rains in may after an early spring bloom in April and I have read of snows in a Moscow summer.

But I read nothing in the Movements of the season or the shifting of days into nights. If anything it is the world's well-hidden mania; the bi-polarity of a too young mother; her entire life devoted to a child she will resent until her dying days; it is madness and the only reason.

And madness is the world's god-sign; the only proof that could ever be of divinity, if one were so inclined, but I am not. I am of the generation reared on deconstruction and have not even faith in things seen; I cannot stretch for that which will forever be unrevealed. At this moment, the lord in a blinding light could reveal himself to me. He could buckle my legs beneath my own weight and open my heart to his wondrous possibility, but my eager mind would no doubt inquire as to his nature. I could come face to face with the lord and not believe a single hair of his white beard or the tenderness of his paternal embrace. I do not have faith.

If he were accommodating, lending himself to inquisition, answering every question he would die. He would pass into oblivion and the history books. He would become to himself only a pleasant notion. He would become for himself as a young man's nostalgic remembrance of Saint Nicholas. He would find in the death of Christ the pronouncement of his own death long before a German philosopher, and he would have to realize his imperfection, his fear of destruction, his fear of not existing, in order to resurrect himself. He would resurrect imperfection.

The lord is madness and inconsistency is his gift to me.

And the twilight hours are his gift to me. These sensual hours of sarongs and under shirts, and the natural perspiration before the dance; it seems as if the women walking in the street, though on their way to the first club, are in fact in the midst of making their rounds and have already danced.

These summer twilight hours, where the night begins in the heart, in the meat of the night; where the men explode in fist fights provoked by the young women who are what seems an eternity removed from the old women they will become; leaning from their window sills, their sagging arms resting on pillows, overlooking the commotion below.

In this is the sadness of the twilight hours; the cessation of vitality, where only the artist's tact and repose to the sublime can rescue the human spirit from suicide. We are aging and the young women are aging as well. The night encourages us, in its poor lighting, to turn a blind eye to this fact and to drink deep everything at our disposal and to curse with merriment, with often-feigned merriment and more the wailing of the condemned, these fleeting moments no net designed can catch and hold; the children's nets are as porous as time.

The men and women, the boys and girls, dance is this lunacy. They dance under the lunar cycles. They howl at the night sky and shriek at one another. They turn deliriously in their frenzied dance to imbibe the evenings through their skin, through their soft skin and firm tendons. They resist in their hearts the weight of the coming dawn that bears on the levity of the evenings and brings the curtain of death sharply down in the form of an empty bed, abandoned in the night by a new lover or the cold bowl of cereal eaten over the sink in an unlit kitchen in the morning.

I cannot escape anymore. I cannot flee the ugly maturation and eventual decay of the flesh. Each dancer gives way, from exhaustion, to another dancer refreshed from having sat for a moment or two; I will not be replaced. I will not be consumed and drowned in the dance with the others. My life is a work of art and its inspiration is my spirit.

I am unapologetic.

I am not a convergence for the currents of history and circumstances. My depths cannot be plumbed, as here in the crossroads of time, the silt is thick and the scientific instruments cannot see their way.

I am of the same metal as all the jutting cliffs and islands that dot the earth's surface and channel the world's waters into another course; my existence is more the volcanoes of the south seas than the drift wood that litters the beaches.

Chapter 5

I am asleep in the apartment across the hall from Alexander. He sleeps in an exaggerated closet, in makeshift pajamas fom an old shirt of mine and his underpants.

In my sleep I have nightmares. I hear from the Recesses a clenched cry; the howl of the counter revolutionary; the cry of the saboteur, the curses of a man subordinating the Structure to his feverish outpourings of discontent.

I am the malcontent.

I am the pharaoh finding in his monuments, his wondrous pyramids, his refutation of mortality and the due course of nature; I am finding in the summit of my ambitions my own grave. And when the final stone is placed upon the pinnacle of my earthly success I will be buried in its basement with the rats.

I am the pugilist in this night teeming with pedestrians all around. I am the boxer in the ring; surrounded; caged in on all sides by the men from the hills and my efforts are chained like a disobedient dog made obedient by muzzle and choke. Kid gloves pad my hands and deny my fists the sweet satisfaction of another's giving cheekbone. The ring limits my Movements and the extent of my activities. There is a fight within me, but my energies seems misdirected with every summation of the judges' cards and every cat call from the stands; I am the public's fighting van Gogh who's suicide is the only thing to bring them to the gallery after the memorial. And I am close enough to only spit in their faces.

They want my suicide.

They want my sabotage. The Movement and the men in the hills; they are asking for it because what I can give is confined to the ring and the back alley where fights are pre-arranged, and the ring sees only a player working from a prompter hovering in the crowd; he is shouting, as a director, "Cut."

In my nightmares, my suicide is as impotent as the pageant in the square.

And the public will applaud my suicide, my corn row death, and they will enter vicariously for curiosities sake into the permanence of my demise and return to their bleachers for the next contest between impotents and the next show in the square.

The pyramids, the fight, the maddeningly beautiful Starry Nights, are all born to the grave and the illusion of sabotaged Structure and the Movement...it all returns to naught. It is despicable. Nothing will come of this, of this counterrevolution save the counter-revolution and it must then be justified in my heart and not my legacy.

I am as a French revolutionary, with colors in hand, storming the Bastille only to find the liberation of Sade and a musket round exploding in my chest. I have given my life in a second for a cause I will not believe in a minute.

And I want desperately to wake up; to taste the sunlight on my tongue and see across from me my son and to believe in the enduring good grace of a man's legacy however cruel. But there is no wake and there is no alarm loud enough to banish from my ears the horrendous cavalcade of men dying around me and the escaping breath from my punctured ribs as I lay dying at the foot of the Bastille; it stands like a monstrous hill and the Sade is my gift to the world.

I want to wake up, and in the murmurings of my lips caught shivering in my final breaths I am trying to impart to Alexander the truth; that I died and nothing more and that my boy should find nothing in his own child to justify such an end. It is not the free Bastille; it is not the vice of freedom; there is no consequence to my actions to justify them; my life is over before the cause is won; the cause is never ours; it is never the soldiers; and there is a great divide between the life of the living and the dead who procured it for them that cannot be traversed; the expanse is too great even for Christ.

I wake, and to my boy's bed I hurriedly clamber in a somnambulant stupor; more awake than I will be when the nightmare is returned to my subconscious and I lift the banner again to convince myself in the counterrevolution and the fall of the Movement and the end of the garbage collector.

"Alexander, wake up."

"What are you doing? Are you drunk? He's sleeping."

"No, I'm not. He's sleeping?"

"Yes."

There is nothing so impenetrable as a clear mind.

The jazz musician is playing as I pour myself into the street.

My limitations are prickly like a porcupines quills. I want to tear them from my flesh and write in this back alley the manifesto of my heart and find it fluid like the ink that runs from the quills tip, but the quills are pronged and irritate the skin; where they are removed infections grow and men die, so the manifesto can never be written.

And I curse the nightmares, that not even in the realm of dreams can my deepest desires be realized. I am always at once on stage, beneath the nimble fingers of my situation, playing out a tune to the expectations of my audience who will one day demand blood in the form of a revolution that they will quickly squelch before I reach the ring in a musket ball exploding from the bleachers at the director's command.

These are desperate hours, hours pleading before the barrel of a gun I cannot see. I am pleading in all directions not knowing what to say or do; nothing will stop the final edit of this horrific film.

If only the horn player would abandon his lyrical massage that dulls the senses and removes the fight and play an unfamiliar tune for the streets; if only he would break into Mendelssohn; if only he would abandon his skin and play the songs of the counterrevolution, thought they are shit, and when he does... I will demand that he play the songs of the black man, as they are the only songs to set us free, perhaps and I want to be free from even this demand to be free.

I am turning corners, staggering in my still water logged cast through the streets of this bastard city and every alley every turn brings me closer to the labyrinths center where the efforts of a man cannot be revived by a well lain spool of thread and the Minotaur of the labyrinth is waiting.

"But I am not a virgin girl! I am not a virgin girl!"

I am shouting into the night that I will not satisfy the Minotaur's appetites and though the crowds are gathered around me and watch with their disposable cameras, as they are on vacation from the hills and far-away places and its all a wonderful picture show of characters.

"These costumes," I confess, "are donned under the pretense of a great escape; I am waiting for a hot air balloon to pass overhead and drop its rope ladder on to which I will cling and be carried over the hills and laugh and drink and be merry in the company of those who were clever; who were strong; who opposed and won and fought to a land where the sun sets when the sun is told and the commands are delivered from the blackness that sits in the gut of every man; and every man has a sun and every man has a son."

I collapse in a seizure. I am not well, but they will leave me here.

In the air above the crowds and the streetcars, I hear Mendelssohn wafting from the hills; the horn player cannot play loud enough and he calls it a night.

Chapter 6

She says my name.

It is raining. I am lying in a fetal position. She found me on her way to work.

"Wake up."

"I was sleeping."

"Were you dreaming?"

"No."

"Pity."

"Really?"

"Dreams are pleasant."

"For who?"

"For me."

It is early morning. My head is heavy. And the waitress is still lovely.

"Let's get you some coffee."

The night is still with me. I am close to tears in her arms. I am grateful for the rain. She does not notice, as I quickly sweep away the emerging tears.

I return to boyhood with her.

I have never left, but I return. She is marmalade on toast and tea with honey; chicken soup even or the promise that I won't have to go to school.   She is every form of certainty and protection I cannot offer.

This is the root of the manhood I will never feel.

Here and now, with her arms wrapped around my still shivering shoulders, I want to tell her everything; and I know the cowardice of such an act and the betrayal that comes with such a burden but still; I want to divulge everything, like a schoolboy before the principal has phoned home. I am racing the telephone. I am racing inside. My mind is an electric current; it's why I have seizures and the storm cloud hovering in my thoughts.   But there is no principal and the silence can remain, but the ingrained principles are the ones that dart through my mind and threaten to reveal myself at an inopportune moment.   These are the thoughts not of the guilty schoolboy, but of the subversive, though the two are one in the same.

I will tell her soon enough, perhaps before we have reached the café; before the coffee has been poured; before the warming effect and the caffeine have taken effect. I will say it first in a whisper; a whisper she will hear and register and not believe entirely. It will be the first volley of fire before the onslaught; before everything she has known of the Movement and myself will be destroyed and she will find a new man huddled before her; the most deformed idealist; the only idealist left, as only in ideals, the ones in my manifesto locked securely in my breast and my ignorant appetites, where every virtue and vice is held, weighed, and placed in my life; it is in these ignorant and autistic appetites that truth finds home.

I want her to love the truth as I love the truth, but only in her love of me could she ever love the truth; truth's salvation is the charisma of its vessel; it is the missionary who shaves every morning though deep on an African savannah. The message, some call it a spirit, is held in the fist and never let go; it is only sworn upon.

As she prepares the cup of coffee, my mind tries to remember last night, but the seizure has erased everything; the nightmare is gone. I am free to commit myself to action as I have forgotten the futility of my course.

She brings the cups of coffee and in gratitude I lean into her and whisper.

The coffee spills.

Her eyes well with tears and she extends a hand over mine.

"The coffee is good thank you."

"You're welcome."

We pass the time in conversation. We do not talk of the counter-revolution. We talk of the weather and her plans for a tiny garden she has managed to grow on her balcony; it is tiny and gets very little light so she must be careful with what she chooses to grow. I don't know gardens and vegetables, but I know her, and like a boy beside his mother as she identifies every herb, though the rains have washed away their tags, I listen intently, as what is said is important to her and she is important to me and the counterrevolution is really a young boy's garden.

My garden does not get enough light, but still I have plans.

Chapter 7

Alexander is waiting. He is sitting on the top step that leads to the apartment. His plastic cup is lying in his lap and his eyes are squinting in the sunlight that only recently broke through the clouds and now is reflected at all angles by the slick pavement below and the rooftops overhead; there is no escaping it.

He looks fresh from a nap. His disheveled hair is the color of ash; the color of premature age; the color of a man who has had too much education. At his age it were better had he only read a lot, but the boy is inquisitive and even when the sun is blinding he opens his eyes. Even when the world is unforgiving he opens his eyes and when his father lies in the position of a still born he never thinks to close them, and this is the curse of children; they do not know to avert their attention.

They breathe deep every exhale of experience and every word. It makes a man wish to speak only moderately, but moderation is of another time; a halcyon day; a vague notion less a memory than a decade some years ago before we were born. We can show the children picture books, but we cannot share with them nostalgia or the sense of security and optimism the years possessed; they were never ours.

We were born into the ill-fated marriage of pragmatism and skepticism, and their bickering was deafening. We were born when the north and south poles collapsed into one another and the scalding equator of an unavoidable sun seized on our vision and cataracted our sight.

His eyes are open and it is all I can do to raise a hand and shield them from the sunlight, if for only a moment.

Before I have to leave.

"Alexander."

Parting words; I am searching for my parting words. The demonstration is today and I do not know its outcome, though I have my designs, but as everything; it only looks good on paper, and so I am searching.

I want to tell him everything I have come to know and that there is nothing to know; knowledge is held to the heart, like a child's first stuffed animal; it is whatever has been offered in the cradle. It is a flat earth, a cheese moon, an egg a day and cancer from a portable phone; Alexander, let no one educate you. They have nothing to say, and even the virtues of freedom are tempered by its vices, and the effect from a cause is significant only if your first memory is of a mathematical function, but if you are hot blooded and dark and don't expect to find truth in reason then look to form and never look too far because you will find its function and vice versa.

Look to justification from the horse's mouth, but make sure he is wearing blinders and is harnessed to a carriage in the touristy part of town because he will lead you astray. If he his not wearing blinders he will see everything at once and he will lead you astray.

I want to tell him, as well, that the theatre is an old profession and his father is tired of removing make-up like a woman after the final curtain call. He is tired of feigning gratitude in a curtsy like bow. He is tired of speaking another man's words and finding his only satisfaction in the dismantling of the set after every run, and yet I want Alexander to know that the English man was right and that all the world's a stage, but I want Alexander to script his own theatre, as I, myself, want to raise to the soil the cities square, so that my boy, my son, will never cartwheel for the deli managers laughing son and the malicious bluebloods who's lisping lips are pressed to the playwrights ears.

And more importantly I need for Alexander to know that I leave him no legacy, and that is my legacy; he is yoked to nothing and burdened by no expectation, as life is vindicated in the heart and not the unforeseeable consequences of living. It is not a crapshoot, Life; it is the die that will never leave your hands. He cannot look to me for expectations, as I expect nothing of him, as a man who moves left or right will return full circle always if he holds to his path and if he wanders? What matter is a full circle.

I will not tell him he will be missed; this goes without saying.

I will educate him by example, as I have always done, like a school marm at the blackboard, the last chapter of our lesson plan is the final exultant contradiction in his father's life.

"Good-bye, Alexander"

He says nothing.

He does not cry.

He does not bat an eye, but only squints again when my hand stops shielding his eyes. He is young to be a man, and I am young to be a boy.

I descend the steps, pass into an alley where cats scavenge from the restaurants waste and begin to sob uncontrollably, thinking to myself that perhaps this has always been the case-a father rearing a boy to manhood never having attained it himself. And here in this back alley, squinting, as the sunlight is everywhere, through the watery fog of my tears I see others like myself; curled in standing positions of supplication; there faces buried in their hands; and before I wipe the tears away they seem to me crying for their own paternal shortcomings; but once my eyes are dried I see they are only the homeless and they are scavenging like cats.

And from the far end of the alley, impossibly silhouetted, like a dark harbinger of doom, the deli manager, with Billy club in hand is beating them down, as he works his way to me and to our scheduled appointment before the demonstration.

Chapter 8

"To what end?"

This from a man who's fingers bleed for an obsession with cleanliness; who recycles beside the bodies of the homeless men he batters, like aged greyhound dogs; who relishes the task at hand, and I know that the question is more a delayed orgasm than true consideration, but I play the tease, as I do need this.

"None."

"To no end?"

"Like everything."

"You won't say that once I'm through with you."

"I suppose not."

But I don't believe him.   Like the Russians, I have long known that man is that creature that can adapt to anything.

"No, you won't.   You'll feel each blow with regret and-"

"Don't stop."

"I won't, but you will want me to."

"Yes."

"To what end?"

And I wonder if he is sufficiently enticed.

"Now."

"To what end?"

To the end of the Movement; to martyrdom without true sacrifice; to a legacy I do not recognize; for the demands of my gut that writhes in frustration and demands, with juvenility, a Pollack-like explosion onto the canvas of the world; finding the brushes and colors of the artist too refined to hold the dumb logic of the spirit.

"I need this battery. It is the end!"

And with this his Billy club, the very club that crushed the skull of the old man and every homeless man's ribs the deli manager ever came across; with this club that tore into the belly of the arthritic dog, scattering its intestines across the dark city street on the night when the counterrevolution was set in motion; when my revolution was begun; this club he brings down onto my shoulder, shattering my collar bone.

And he begins anew. All the while demanding to know whether I wish him to stop and of course I do.

I am screaming.

"Enough!"

With every blow, every fracture, every ounce of blood that leaves my body- he is a strip miner this deli manager, and I want him to stop; I want him to stop, but he is an atomic reaction and the bunker is a thin channel in the earth reinforced with wooden planks, and he cannot be dissuaded as he mushrooms against the sky, radiating fear, turning the sand on the street to glass and burning my shadow into the alley.

He continues with a factories dedication and the Sade's thrill. He churns with a mechanical momentum. He coughs up through smoke stacks oil filth that rains down on me, the town below, and works into my wounds like black vinegar.

And like a factory he continues long after the product has fallen into disfavor and I feel the foolish governmental agency that subsidized his archaic industry.

He is finished. He is swaying. He is drunk on the task and cannot lift his arms above his head, but rather rests them on his engorged belly where I see he has grown content with his self-actualization; his belly looks as a twin he absorbed in the womb and each rub carries reminiscence of two congratulatory brothers.

It did not take long for him to adapt to himself and as I lie here, as I work my toothless gums, flowing with blood, with my tongue bleeding from the times when I had teeth and they could bite down in agony; I remember the Russians and what they know and I remember the French.

The deli manager is sleeping like a baby.

I am falling unconscious and adapting as well, and perhaps this is the only thing that is not acceptable, and I think that the French are a wise people.

Chapter 9

I wake to the commotion in the square. It has already begun and I can tell by the pitch of the chants that the Movement is riled and waiting for a spark. From the alley I can see the square. The military police follow the procession of "activists" and artists. They keep a distance behind, their helmets slung from their belts, Billy clubs holstered, and wearing the padding of an American football player; they are waiting for the spark.

Ambulances follow behind the line of officers and the officers' vehicles; they are there for the cities protection, for the Movement's protection and for the police whom everyone blames for the old man's death and the incidents of last week; of the last protest, though we all know the truth. It is a reality not acknowledged. It is an unattractive debutante flattered to tears as the room and the boys know the truth.

The street sweepers are visible. They are picking up the garbage of the Movement, shattering glass bottles on the sidewalks and then clearing it all into the path of the cities large street cleaning trucks. Though in the past they have eradicated all remembrances of the demonstrations, today, however, they will serve a different function. A capacity I cannot speak for, save its distinctions; they will serve a different function.

The garbage collector, the discorsi di the garbage collector, is carried to the mass assembled via a loudspeaker hanging from the back of a truck. Intermittently his speeches give way for the "free radio" of the Movement's non-governmental radio station and its propaganda, which today entails, among ska recordings and thrash metal, actual demands on the part of the Movement for the prosecution of the murderous officer.

The deli manager has not seen me rise to my feet. He is sleeping still.

The deli manager conceded to not bludgeon my head with such "vigor," as I needed my wits about me. He was remorseful, but compliant; I passed out for the pain, thankfully, and not any severe debilitation. Remarkably, I can walk.

Supporting myself on the alleys walls, I hobble, my legs shaking as if from Parkinson's, to the open of the square where it meets the alley. The atmosphere is thick with the righteousness of the protestors and the righteousness of the military police, and I feel as though, in having passed from the alley, I have left the imperfections of the deli manager, gluttonous and corpulent, to a heaven of sorts where righteousness, if only briefly, exists in every heart.

It will not last and I wonder if such is the case with every heaven.

Were my collarbone not broken I would look to the sky.

As it is I can lift my head only so much to see the waitress standing beside the garbage collector. Her eyes are darting through the crowd from face to face looking for me and when she finds me; when she sees me leaning against the alley wall; her hesitant breath; the flush of her face; her disbelief, timed with the precision of the planets, reveals my location to the garbage collector who turns to find out what is wrong.

His disgust is a poor charade; he is a witch hunter playing dissatisfied for having found his faggots soaked in oil. I have only been a bundle of wood to him, as I have only been the Movement's puppet; its player. He incites the crowd to assist me, as the truck, the conspicuous truck will drive me to hospital, and from here, as I am hoisted and well-received he grabs the loud speakers' hand set and sets me on fire.

And the protestors seem dancing now through the flames on a black Sabbath on a hot summer day.

Admirably, without forethought, holding the loud speakers' receiver to my mouth, he asks, "who? who did this?"

The crowd is silent. The beach balls from past demonstrations are missing; it is less a rally than a powder keg, and the electrified receiver in my hand soaked in blood is a detonating device.

A great London fog.

A lone paddleboat drifting in an otherwise empty pond.

A child's ball dropped and left behind for the evening, slowly; falling; motionless.

A still dense expanse of humanity. Like Christ I could walk across it. I could stir its waters. I could reveal the truth of the deli manager's proclivities and temper the storm with a word, but My truth would be drowned.

And the death of the Movement from here seems a work of art; a sculpture in which time and space are unified; where the eyes wanders seamlessly around the square, as there is nothing from the piece to disrupt the eyes. There is only the vantage point of the artist and what he has designed from his own desires and needs; from the black recesses of his spirit where he finds his truth; the truth before education; the truth of his perception unmolested by sensation.

All the world is a stage, and a marionette stage at that.

The question is asked again.

The phrase is piece de-resistance.

And my convictions shatter the stillness that had formed, like the arrogant chisel of Michelangelo emblazoning his signature across the pieta; the sounds rupture, like chinks of marble from the Virgin Mary's robe.

I have done this, they scream into the face of the crowd and the men on the hill.

"A police officer."

An explosion.

The first Molotov cocktail is thrown and the crowd erupts. Behind banners and from coat pockets incendiary devices are launched in the direction of the military police. Most bottles explode a few yards from the police lines, but one or two hit their targets head on and policemen bleed; the bottles have been rolled in nails and scrap metal. They take off like shrapnel.

Rubber bullets are dispersed and protestors fall with shattered bones and jaws. A woman has lost her eye. The onlookers have already rushed for cover; towards the hills where they will hole up in their homes and watch from their balconies overlooking the valley.

The "free radio" truck careens through the square. The garbage collector anticipated a riot and the truck is well stocked; the bohemian s are handing out to the teenagers and thugs in bandanas stones large enough to maim, yet small enough to hurl. Not a few cocktails make there way into the eager hands of the jean clad boys.

The Bedouin women have surprisingly good arms.

A cry from the crowd; an officer is dead. Touché'!

And for fear of a loss of momentum the garbage collector recoils and hurls into the crowd a police style grenade. Three young women are seriously injured and one will die a timely death; she will die soon enough.

Suspicions in the truck are that the police are already drawing straws for more martyrs. Provisions are made within our own ranks to fill the Party's quota; to keep step with the opposition. Names are volunteered, but in the fog of battle the garbage collector demonstrates himself a decisive man and selects from the Bedouin women who surround the truck. A faulty cocktail; a short fuse; all ensure the casualties needed to sustain the Movement.

The jolts from hurtling through the square send me crashing to the trucks bed. The waitress attends to my injuries with the care of a nurse. From all around I hear the sirens, though in the trucks bed I see only the canopy strewn with slogans and the blue sky breaking through its holes; new holes; live fire.

It was only a matter of time.

He doesn't feel it. It happens suddenly, like sleep; the exact moment lost in reflection, yet still very real. He is the first, and a great strategic error. The garbage collector is slumping to his knees. The truck is grinding to a halt, and the crowd is left to their passions, as the voice of their Movement, their only stake in reason, is dead.

I have heard stories of the bodies of men guillotined rising from the doctor's device and searching madly for their head still blinking in a basket; the great body of the Movement is on hands and knees fumbling around for the kings head.

The king is dead.

Of the four large poles on the trucks body that support the canopy and slogans, I hold fast to one and hoist my decrepit body, as a mast, more as a flag, to the receiver feeding into the loud speakers.

The king is dead; long live the king.

The live rounds have stopped, and only the occasional rubber bullet finds its way into the protestors. Its as if the police have left us a dramatic moment to come to terms, to access our decapitation and capitulate; to feel the breeze stir across the napes of our necks and to feel the days finiteness as the Movements.

They are mistaken.

If they are right in any respect it is the significance of the garbage collector; he was not just a figurehead. He was the orator from the pulpit. He was the crowd's father; their priest; their moral compass and absolving force on earth. It was he who made crimes permissible, but with his death the crimes do not lose their appeal.

The garbage collector was not a figurehead, and the crowd is not his creation; it is a tool. The Movement is its figurehead.

It is my flag and it has touched the ground.

I am sending it to the hills to be burned.

Chapter 10

The "free radio" is in my hands.

There is no speech prepared. There is no pomp; only circumstance. The Movement knows only circumstance.

"He is dead. Take it to the hills."

And the Moloch rises; its belly arched like a cat at once terrified and aggressive and perhaps hydrophobic. The deli manager is operating inside the bowels as the china men dance and the stolen paper towel roll is replaced.

The Moloch, pacified in the square, heaves but does not retreat. The boys throwing stones advance, but now do not withdraw and the motions of the Moloch today in the square are more than the inhalation and exhalations of a sleeping giant; they are a revolution, an exultant revolution of my own design, furthering my own ends leading to its own ruin; my victory.

And this generation of functional suicidals is quick to raise my banner without question. These still borns, miscarried into the world, mishandled by their education, by every romantic educator who expounded the meritorious satanic figure, the Byronic hero, and then denied them their orgies and base gratification; that stripped from their city the opium dens and left only the memory in text books without disclaimers. No matter the police are here to decide what is right or wrong, as no one would ever burn a book.

No, for the generation looking for their liberty and individual determination it is best they burn people. Or at least blind them with non-lethal force. There's an education.

Is this a natural conclusion then?

I have resisted the natural conclusion at every step, so that I might exist. I found myself caught up in a swift undercurrent and paddled furiously to resist, so that I might determine my own course. I have sent the Movement to the hills where the Charlton Hestons wait with stocked armories and voracious appetites for the task at hand, so that I might stand author and not character, but the flood of protestors charging the hills, from a distance, merge into a swarm, and seem very much to me, like a white crest carried on an oceans wave to the very natural conclusion of dissipation on the beach.

The teenage boys trampling rhododendrons and shrieking through sprinklers like young bathing suit clad, formless girls in pig tails; the stones hurled through windows with the mischievous indifference of the sexually frustrated; the gasoline tanks siphoned of gasoline and the tires punctured with a boy's Swiss army knife hand-me-down from a brother on rampage the street over; it seems to my eyes no more spectacular than events in the square the week before. The intensity and the location are changed, but I wonder if this pseudo-individuation is more a fabulous performance troupe in a change of venue.

And the greatest fear I have is that I did not wake the Moloch, but only arranged a simple tour for the players.

Gunshots.

The killing begins.

And I sigh a sigh of relief as the players have forgotten their lines, the curtains are drawn at inappropriate moments, and exits are made with disgusting and comical over stylization; the Movement is dying and in the pit, I, the conductor, need not conduct anymore, but simply wait my turn to graciously accept my applause from an audience who has never seen the likes and will never again.

I am an original, a maestro and the dead boys; the dead Bedouins; the dead castratos are a sight not soon forgotten, but the true joy of the endeavor has been the intense sense of personal satisfaction, as what is a legacy to a dead man?

"Are you satisfied?" she asks.

"Yes."

"To what end? Accolades?"

"Accolades are for the actors. I make music!"

"The actors are dead."

"The actors are dying. Look there, Mr. Heston has yet to reach that young man."

"His eyesight's poor."

"The boy's"

"Hestons"

"Must get close then? Point blank? Heston is a fine player!"

I am pleased I have chosen such a fine cast: the tragically flawed Jimmy Deans and the exceptional villains of Heston.

"Predictable."
"No!"
Only I saw this coming. Only I knew the end.

Chapter 11

Overlooking the now empty city square, from the vantage point of his high-rise office, the grandfather of the town finally rests his knees. He permits the three-legged Table to fall to the floor; there is no one left to make concessions to.

His grandchildren are called in from the adjoining room and tea is prepared by the children's mother.

"My legs are old," he grumbles as he twists the knees in preparation to stand.

"Be careful now grandfather."

"Don't worry yourselves about me."

His Movements are stilted at first, as if his legs were the trunks of California oaks to complement his rosy cheeks; the sound of leather fills the large room that's more a reconfigured hall; used to accentuate the old man's stature, both physical and social.

He's a full moustache that's noticeably well trimmed.

He shot five castratos from his window, from behind the Table. He would mount them if the boys wouldn't clash with the décor.

I enter from the study. I have not been kept waiting.

"Maestro!"

"Sir."

"A remarkable show. Bully!"

"Thank you."

A cup of tea is handed me from the delicate and porcelain hands of his daughter, the mother of the children.

"Yes, maestro; very well performed."

"Sugar."

"No thank you."

"Now, one thing particularly-"

"Cream?"

"Yes."

"When?"

"When. Thank you."

"I'm sorry dear you were asking the maestro something."

"Yes...oh I've forgotten."

"One thing in particular?"

"In particular...yes!"

"In particular..."

"What becomes of the maestro?"

"Yes, bully question I was just wondering that myself."

"Well, I don't want to spoil the ending."

"Do tell! You can tell us."

"Rather."

"I believe you, in fact. It might be best for my legacy if I do confide in you."

"Good."

"More tea?"

"Maestro...you're stalling!"

"Oh very well than! Over a cigar!"

"A fine cohiba robusto!"

"Now! I insist."

"Very well!...I...am...poisoned."

"With what?"

"Can you keep a secret?"

"No"

"Good. With tea."

"By whom?"

"Is that necessary?"

"Terribly sorry."

"Is it painful, Father."

"I hope not."

"It shouldn't be"

"Excellent…lovely cigar."

"Maestro."

"Yes?"

"Last words?"

"First…you'll need this address…she's a waitress…tell her it was all my design…my little garden."

"Yes…thank you.   We were having trouble finding her."

"Maestro?"

"Last words…right…"

"Take your time."

"Something memorable, as a legacy is important…sometimes…"

"…are those they?"

"I can feel it working."

"You best sit down."

"Here."

"Oh not there.   I'll look like some dreadful Ibsen syphilitic!"

"Have you a preference?"

"Among the children."

"Very well."

"Last words?"

"...in a second...I have given my life in a second for a cause I will not believe in a minute..."

"Very clever."

"Good-bye."

And with this I pass. The time of my death is noted and the children are permitted to play with my still warm body for another half hour.   Another thirty minutes the grandfather feels would be too "macabre."

My last words are recorded as "good-bye."

Printed in the United States
1520600001B/250-264